Good-bye, Mr. Chips,

and Other Stories

Good-bye, Mr. Chips

and Other Stories

James Hilton

ILLUSTRATIONS BY DONNA DIAMOND

THE WORLD'S BEST READING

The Reader's Digest Association, Inc.
Pleasantville, N.Y • Montreal

Good-bye, Mr. Chips
and Other Stories

This Reader's Digest edition contains the complete text of
James Hilton's *Good-bye, Mr. Chips,*
first published in 1934, and selected short stories from
To You, Mr. Chips, first published in 1938.

Contents

Illustrations

81

"You cannot—umph—judge the importance of
things—umph—by the noise they make."

109

He threw a piece of inky paper while
Mr. Pearson's back was turned.

124

Menvers, in that stuffy courtroom, provided the sole
focus of anything even remotely aligned to humanity.

143

"I've been trying to make a bonfire. . . . I wanted
to rouse the burglars of Carlisle."

153

It was Chips who had given her the
scoop about Randolph Renny.

177

Attwood Primus . . . suddenly fainted . . .
slipping to the floor with a reverberating crash.

180

"You'll join me, Mrs. Wickett, in—umph—
a glass of wine?"

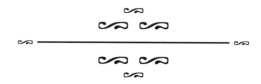

ood-bye, Mr. Chips was written in London during a foggy week of November 1933. I am chary of using the word "inspiration," which is too often something nonexistent that a writer waits for when he is lazy; but, as a matter of record, *Good-bye, Mr. Chips* was written more quickly, more easily, and with fewer subsequent alterations than anything I had ever written before, or have ever written since.

It was first published in the Christmas number of the *British Weekly,* in December 1933; after which, with a certain wild abandon, I had it sent to the *Atlantic Monthly*—a magazine which I had long held as a secret pinnacle of ambition. The *Atlantic* printed the story in its issue of April 1934, and about the same time proposed its publication as a book. This publication took place on June 8. Four months later *Good-bye, Mr. Chips* first appeared as a book in England, from Messrs. Hodder and Stoughton. Thus one may summarize that, having been written and first printed in its native land, it was discovered by America, and later came back to England with the success that America had given it. And now, again in America, it appears in this new and sumptuous dress.

If I recount these details with pride, I do so also with modesty, for I know how few are the writers to whom such romances happen, and that, with no matter how much or little merit, a portion of luck must be distilled. But I do take pride in the reception that America has given to my very English book; certainly no author could ever have enjoyed his correspondence more than I have during the past year. One feature has been the discovery of the original Mr. Chips in so many different parts of the world; and I believe those letters from readers have told the whole truth, and that my tribute to a great profession has fitted a great many members of it everywhere.

J. H.

Wanstead, London
March 1935

When you are getting on in years (but not ill, of course), you get very sleepy at times, and the hours seem to pass like lazy cattle moving across a landscape. It was like that for Chips as the autumn term progressed and the days shortened till it was actually dark enough to light the gas before call-over. For Chips, like some old sea captain, still measured time by the signals of the past; and well he might, for he lived at Mrs. Wickett's, just across the road from the School.

He had been there more than a decade, ever since he finally gave up his mastership; and it was Brookfield far more than Greenwich time that both he and his landlady kept. "Mrs. Wickett," Chips would sing out, in that jerky, high-pitched voice that had still a good deal of sprightliness in it, "you might bring me a cup of tea before prep, will you?"

When you are getting on in years it is nice to sit by the fire and drink a cup of tea and listen to the school bell sounding dinner, call-over, prep, and lights-out. Chips always wound up the clock after that last bell; then he put the wire guard in front of the fire, turned out the gas, and carried a detective novel to bed. Rarely did he read more than a page of it before sleep came swiftly and peacefully, more like a mystic intensifying of perception than any changeful entrance into another world. For his days and nights were equally full of dreaming.

He was getting on in years (but not ill, of course); indeed, as Doctor Merivale said, there was really nothing the matter with him. "My dear fellow, you're fitter than I am," Merivale would say, sipping a glass of sherry when he called every fortnight or so. "You're past the age when people get these horrible diseases; you're one of the few lucky ones who're going to die a really natural death. That is, of course, if you die at all. You're such a remarkable old boy that one never knows." But when Chips had a cold or when east winds roared over the fenlands, Merivale would sometimes take Mrs. Wickett aside in the lobby and whisper: "Look after him, you know. His chest . . . it puts a strain on his heart. Nothing really wrong with him—only anno domini, but that's the most fatal complaint of all, in the end."

Anno domini . . . by Jove, yes. Born in 1848, and taken to the Great Exhibition as a toddling child—not many people still alive could boast a thing like that. Besides, Chips could even remember Brookfield in Wetherby's time. A phenomenon, that was. Wetherby had been an old man in those days—1870—easy to remember because of the Franco-Prussian War. Chips had put in for Brookfield after a year at Melbury, which he hadn't liked, because he had been ragged there a good deal. But Brookfield he *had* liked, almost from the beginning. He remembered that day of his preliminary interview—sunny June, with the air full of flower scents and the plick-plock of cricket on the pitch. Brookfield was playing Barnhurst, and one of the Barnhurst boys, a chubby little fellow, made a brilliant century. Queer that a thing like that should stay in the memory so clearly. Wetherby himself was very fatherly and courteous; he must have been ill then, poor chap, for he died during the summer vacation, before Chips began his first term. But the two had seen and spoken to each other, anyway.

Chips often thought, as he sat by the fire at Mrs. Wickett's: I am probably the only man in the world who has a vivid recollection of old Wetherby. . . . Vivid, yes; it was a frequent picture in his mind, that summer day with the sunlight filtering through the dust in Wetherby's study. "You are a young man, Mr. Chipping, and Brookfield is an old foundation. Youth and age often combine well. Give your enthusiasm to Brookfield, and Brookfield will give you something in return. And don't let anyone play tricks with you. I—er—gather that discipline was not always your strong point at Melbury?"

"Well, no, perhaps not, sir."

"Never mind; you're full young; it's largely a matter of experience. You have another chance here. Take up a firm attitude from the beginning—that's the secret of it."

Perhaps it was. He remembered that first tremendous ordeal of taking prep; a September sunset more than half a century ago; Big Hall full of lusty barbarians ready to pounce on him as their legitimate prey. His youth, fresh-complexioned, high-collared, and side-whiskered (odd fashions people followed in those days), at the mercy of five hundred unprincipled ruffians to whom the baiting of new masters was a fine art, an exciting sport, and something of a tradition. Decent little beggars individually, but, as a mob, just pitiless and implacable. The sudden hush as he took his place at the desk on the dais; the scowl he assumed to cover his inward nervousness; the tall clock ticking behind him, and the smells of ink and varnish; the last blood-red rays slanting in slabs through the stained-glass windows. Someone dropped a desk lid. Quickly, he must take everyone by surprise; he must show that there was no nonsense about him. "You there in the fifth row—you with the red hair—what's your name?" "Colley, sir." "Very well, Colley, you have a hundred lines." No trouble at all after that. He had won his first round.

And years later, when Colley was an alderman of the City of London and a baronet and various other things, he sent his son (also red-haired) to Brookfield, and Chips would say: "Colley, your father was the first boy I ever punished when I came here twenty-five years ago. He deserved it then, and you deserve it now." How they all

As Chips sat by his fire with autumn gales rattling the windows, the waves of humor and sadness swept over him.

laughed; and how Sir Richard laughed when his son wrote home the story in next Sunday's letter!

And again, years after that, many years after that, there was an even better joke. For another Colley had just arrived—son of the Colley who was a son of the first Colley. And Chips would say, punctuating his remarks with that little "umph-um" that had by then become a habit with him: "Colley, you are—umph—a splendid example of—umph—inherited traditions. I remember your grandfather—umph—he could never grasp the Ablative Absolute. A stupid fellow, your grandfather. And your father, too—umph—I remember him—he used to sit at that far desk by the wall—he wasn't much better, either. But I do believe—my dear Colley—that you are—umph—the biggest fool of the lot!" Roars of laughter.

A great joke, this growing old—but a sad joke, too, in a way. And as Chips sat by his fire with autumn gales rattling the windows, the waves of humor and sadness swept over him very often until tears fell, so that when Mrs. Wickett came in with his cup of tea she did not know whether he had been laughing or crying. And neither did Chips himself.

Chapter 2

*A*cross the road behind a rampart of ancient elms lay Brookfield, russet under its autumn mantle of creeper. A group of eighteenth-century buildings centred upon a quadrangle, and there were acres of playing fields beyond; then came the small dependent village and the open fen country. Brookfield, as Wetherby had said, was an old foundation; established in the reign of Elizabeth, as a grammar school, it might, with better luck, have become as famous as Harrow. Its luck, however, had been not so good; the School went up and down, dwindling almost to non-existence at one time, becoming almost illustrious at another. It was during one of these latter periods, in the reign of the first George, that the main structure had been rebuilt and large additions made. Later, after the Napoleonic Wars and until mid-Victorian days, the School declined again, both in numbers and in repute. Wetherby, who came in 1840, restored its fortunes somewhat; but its subsequent history never raised it to front-rank status.

It was, nevertheless, a good school of the second rank. Several notable families supported it; it supplied fair samples of the history-making men of the age—judges, members of parliament, colonial administrators, a few peers and bishops. Mostly, however, it turned out merchants, manufacturers, and professional men, with a good sprinkling of country squires and parsons. It was the sort of school which, when mentioned, would sometimes make snobbish people confess that they rather thought they had heard of it.

But if it had not been this sort of school it would probably not have taken Chips. For Chips, in any social or academic sense, was just as respectable, but no more brilliant, than Brookfield itself.

It had taken him some time to realize this, at the beginning. Not that he was boastful or conceited, but he had been, in his early twenties, as ambitious as most other young men at such an age. His dream had been to get a headship eventually, or at any rate a senior mastership in a really first-class school; it was only gradually, after repeated trials and failures, that he realized the inadequacy of his qualifications. His degree, for instance, was not particularly good, and his discipline, though good enough and improving, was not absolutely reliable under all conditions. He had no private means and no family connections of any importance. About 1880, after he had been at Brookfield a decade, he began to recognize that the odds were heavily against his being able to better himself by moving elsewhere; but about that time, also, the possibility of staying where he was began to fill a comfortable niche in his mind. At forty, he was rooted, settled, and quite happy. At fifty, he was the doyen of the staff. At sixty, under a new and youthful Head, he *was* Brookfield—the guest of honor at Old Brookfeldian dinners, the court of appeal in all matters affecting Brookfield history and traditions. And in 1913, when he turned sixty-five, he retired, was presented with a check and a writing desk and a clock, and went across the road to live at Mrs. Wickett's. A decent career, decently closed; three cheers for old Chips, they all shouted, at that uproarious end-of-term dinner.

Three cheers, indeed; but there was more to come, an unguessed epilogue, an encore played to a tragic audience.

Chapter 3

*I*t was a small but very comfortable and sunny room that Mrs. Wickett let to him. The house itself was ugly and pretentious; but that didn't matter. It was convenient—that was the main thing. For he liked, if the weather were mild enough, to stroll across to the playing fields in an afternoon and watch the games. He liked to smile and exchange a few words with the boys when they touched their caps to him. He made a special point of getting to know all the new boys and having them to tea with him during their first term. He always ordered a walnut cake with pink icing from Reddaway's, in the village, and during the winter term there were crumpets, too—a little pile of them in front of the fire, soaked in butter so that the bottom one lay in a little shallow pool. His guests found it fun to watch him make tea—mixing careful spoonfuls from different caddies. And he would ask the new boys where they lived, and if they had family connections at Brookfield. He kept watch to see that their plates were never empty, and punctually at five, after the session had lasted an hour, he would glance at the clock and say: "Well—umph—it's been very delightful—umph—meeting you like this—umph—I'm sorry—umph—you can't stay. . . ." And he would smile and shake hands with them in the porch, leaving them to race across the road to the School with their comments. "Decent old boy, Chips. Gives you a jolly good tea, anyhow, and you *do* know when he wants you to push off. . . ."

And Chips also would be making his comments—to Mrs. Wickett when she entered his room to clear away the remains of the party. "A most—umph—interesting time, Mrs. Wickett. Young Branksome tells me—umph—that his uncle was Major Collingwood—the Collingwood we had here in—umph—nought-two, I think it was. Dear me, I remember Collingwood very well. I once thrashed him—umph—for climbing onto the gymnasium roof—to get a ball out of the gutter. Might have—umph—broken his neck, the young fool. Do you remember him, Mrs. Wickett? He must have been in your time."

Mrs. Wickett, before she saved money, had been in charge of the linen room at the School.

"Yes, I knew 'im, sir. Cheeky, 'e was to me, gener'ly. But we never 'ad no bad words between us. Just cheeky-like. 'E never meant no harm. That kind never does, sir. Wasn't it 'im that got the medal, sir?"

"Yes, a D.S.O."

"Will you be wanting anything else, sir?"

"Nothing more now—umph—till chapel time. He was

killed—in Egypt, I think. . . . Yes—umph—you can bring my supper about then."

"Very good, sir."

A pleasant, placid life, at Mrs. Wickett's. He had no worries; his pension was adequate, and there was a little money saved up besides. He could afford everything and anything he wanted. His room was furnished simply and with schoolmasterly taste: a few bookshelves and sporting trophies; a mantelpiece crowded with fixture cards and signed photographs of boys and men; a worn Turkey carpet; big easy chairs; pictures on the wall of the Acropolis and the Forum. Nearly everything had come out of his old housemaster's room in School House. The books were chiefly classical, the classics having been his subject; there was, however, a seasoning of history and belles-lettres. There was also a bottom shelf piled up with cheap editions of detective novels. Chips enjoyed these. Sometimes he took down Vergil or Xenophon and read for a few moments, but he was soon back again with Doctor Thorndyke or Inspector French. He was not, despite his long years of assiduous teaching, a very profound classical scholar; indeed, he thought of Latin and Greek far more as dead languages from which English gentlemen ought to know a few quotations than as living tongues that had ever been spoken by living people. He liked those short leading articles in the *Times* that introduced a few tags that he recognized. To be among the dwindling number of people who understood such things was to him a kind of secret and valued freemasonry; it represented, he felt, one of the chief benefits to be derived from a classical education.

So there he lived, at Mrs. Wickett's, with his quiet enjoyments of reading and talking and remembering; an old man, white-haired and only a little bald, still fairly active for his years, drinking tea, receiving callers, busying himself with corrections for the next edition of the Brookfeldian Directory, writing his occasional letters in thin, spidery, but very legible script. He had new masters to tea, as well as new boys. There were two of them that autumn term, and as they were leaving after their visit one of them commented: "Quite a character, the old boy, isn't he? All that fuss about mixing the tea—a typical bachelor, if ever there was one."

Which was oddly incorrect; because Chips was not a bachelor at all. He had married; though it was so long ago that none of the staff at Brookfield could remember his wife.

There came to him, stirred by the warmth of the fire and the gentle aroma of tea, a thousand tangled recollections of old times. Spring—the spring of 1896. He was forty-eight—an age at which a permanence of habits begins to be predictable. He had just been appointed housemaster; with this and his classical forms, he had made for himself a warm and busy corner of life. During the summer vacation he went up to the Lake District with Rowden, a colleague; they walked and climbed for a week, until Rowden had to leave suddenly on some family business. Chips stayed on alone at Wasdale Head, where he boarded in a small farmhouse.

One day, climbing on Great Gable, he noticed a girl waving excitedly from a dangerous-looking ledge. Thinking she was in difficulties, he hastened toward her, but in doing so slipped himself and wrenched his ankle. As it turned out, she was not in difficulties at all, but was merely signaling to a friend farther down the mountain; she was an expert climber, better even than Chips, who

He had not . . . expected to find a woman on Great Gable.

was pretty good. Thus he found himself the rescued instead of the rescuer; and neither role was one for which
he had much relish. For he did not, he would have said,
care for women; he never felt at home or at ease with
them; and that monstrous creature beginning to be talked
about, the New Woman of the nineties, filled him with
horror. He was a quiet, conventional person, and the
world, viewed from the haven of Brookfield, seemed to
him full of distasteful innovations; there was a fellow
named Bernard Shaw who had the strangest and most
reprehensible opinions; there was Ibsen, too, with his dis-
turbing plays; and there was this new craze for bicycling
which was being taken up by women equally with men.
Chips did not hold with all this modern newness and
freedom. He had a vague notion, if he ever formulated
it, that nice women were weak, timid, and delicate, and
that nice men treated them with a polite but rather distant chivalry. He had not, therefore, expected to find a
woman on Great Gable; but, having encountered one who
seemed to need masculine help, it was even more terri-
fying that she should turn the tables by helping him. For
she did. She and her friend had to. He could scarcely
walk, and it was a hard job getting him down the steep
track to Wasdale.

Her name was Katherine Bridges; she was twenty-five—
young enough to be Chips's daughter. She had blue, flash-
ing eyes and freckled cheeks and smooth straw-colored
hair. She too was staying at a farm, on holiday with a girl-

friend, and as she considered herself responsible for Chips's accident, she used to bicycle along the side of the lake to the house in which the quiet, middle-aged, serious-looking man lay resting.

That was how she thought of him at first. And he, because she rode a bicycle and was unafraid to visit a man alone in a farmhouse sitting room, wondered vaguely what the world was coming to. His sprain put him at her mercy, and it was soon revealed to him how much he might need that mercy. She was a governess out of a job, with a little money saved up; she read and admired Ibsen; she believed that women ought to be admitted to the universities; she even thought they ought to have a vote. In politics she was a radical, with leanings toward the views of people like Bernard Shaw and William Morris. All her ideas and opinions she poured out to Chips during those summer afternoons at Wasdale Head; and he, because he was not very articulate, did not at first think it worthwhile to contradict them. Her friend went away, but she stayed; what *could* you do with such a person, Chips thought. He used to hobble with sticks along a footpath leading to the tiny church; there was a stone slab on the wall, and it was comfortable to sit down, facing the sunlight and the green-brown majesty of the Gable and listening to the chatter of—well, yes, Chips had to admit it—a very beautiful girl.

He had never met anyone like her. He had always thought that the modern type, this "new woman" business, would repel him; and here she was, making him positively look forward to the glimpse of her safety bicycle careering along the lakeside road. And she, too, had never met anyone like *him*. She had always thought that middle-aged men who read the *Times* and disapproved of modernity were terrible bores; yet here he was, claiming her interest and attention far more than youths of her own age. She liked him, initially, because he was so hard to get to know, because he had gentle and quiet manners, because his opinions dated from those utterly impossible seventies and eighties and even earlier—yet were, for all that, so thoroughly honest; and because—because his eyes were brown and he looked charming when he smiled. "Of course, *I* shall call you Chips, too," she said, when she learned that was his nickname at school.

Within a week they were head over heels in love; before Chips could walk without a stick, they considered themselves engaged; and they were married in London a week before the beginning of the autumn term.

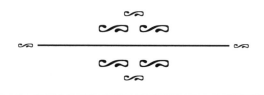

Chapter 5

When Chips, dreaming through the hours at Mrs. Wickett's, recollected those days, he used to look down at his feet and wonder which one it was that had performed so signal a service. That, the trivial cause of so many momentous happenings, was the one thing of which details evaded him. But he resaw the glorious hump of the Gable (he had never visited the Lake District since), and the mouse-gray depths of Wastwater under the Screes; he could resmell the washed air after heavy rain, and refollow the ribbon of the pass across to Sty Head. So clearly it lingered, that time of dizzy happiness, those evening strolls by the waterside, her cool voice and her gay laughter. She had been a very happy person, always.

They had both been so eager, planning a future together; but he had been rather serious about it, even a little awed. It would be all right, of course, her coming to Brookfield; other housemasters were married. And she liked boys, she told him, and would enjoy living among them. "Oh, Chips, I'm so glad you are what you are. I was afraid you were a solicitor or a stockbroker or a dentist or a man with a big cotton business in Manchester. When I first met you, I mean. Schoolmastering's so different, so important, don't you think? To be influencing those who are going to grow up and matter to the world . . ."

Chips said he hadn't thought of it like that—or, at least, not often. He did his best; that was all anyone could do in any job.

"Yes, of course, Chips. I do love you for saying simple things like that."

And one morning—another memory gem-clear when he turned to it—he had for some reason been afflicted with an acute desire to depreciate himself and all his attainments. He had told her of his only mediocre degree, of his occasional difficulties of discipline, of the certainty that he would never get a promotion, and of his complete ineligibility to marry a young and ambitious girl. And at the end of it all she had laughed in answer.

She had no parents and was married from the house of an aunt in Ealing. On the night before the wedding, when Chips left the house to return to his hotel, she said, with mock gravity: "This is an occasion, you know—this last farewell of ours. I feel rather like a new boy beginning his first term with you. Not scared, mind you—but just, for once, in a thoroughly respectful mood. Shall I call you 'sir'—or would 'Mr. Chips' be the right thing?

'Mr. Chips,' I think. Good-bye, then—good-bye, Mr. Chips. . . ."

(A hansom clop-clopping in the roadway; green-pale gas lamps flickering on a wet pavement; newsboys shouting something about South Africa; Sherlock Holmes in Baker Street.)

"Good-bye, Mr. Chips. . . ."

here had followed then a time of such happiness
that Chips, remembering it long afterward,
hardly believed it could ever have happened
before or since in the world. For his marriage was a tri-
umphant success. Katherine conquered Brookfield as she
had conquered Chips; she was immensely popular with
boys and masters alike. Even the wives of the masters,
tempted at first to be jealous of one so young and lovely,
could not long resist her charms.

But most remarkable of all was the change she made
in Chips. Till his marriage he had been a dry and rather
neutral sort of person; liked and thought well of by Brookfield in general, but not of the stuff that makes for great
popularity or that stirs great affection. He had been at
Brookfield for over a quarter of a century, long enough
to have established himself as a decent fellow and a hard
worker; but just too long for anyone to believe him ca-
pable of ever being much more. He had, in fact, already
begun to sink into that creeping dry rot of pedagogy which

is the worst and ultimate pitfall of the profession; giving the same lessons year after year had formed a groove into which the other affairs of his life adjusted themselves with insidious ease. He worked well; he was conscientious; he was a fixture that gave service, satisfaction, confidence, everything except inspiration.

And then came this astonishing girl-wife whom nobody had expected—least of all Chips himself. She made him, to all appearances, a new man; though most of the newness was really a warming to life of things that were old, imprisoned, and unguessed. His eyes gained sparkle; his mind, which was adequately if not brilliantly equipped, began to move more adventurously. The one thing he had always had, a sense of humor, blossomed into a sudden richness to which his years lent maturity. He began to feel a greater sureness; his discipline improved to a point at which it could become, in a sense, less rigid; he became more popular. When he had first come to Brookfield he had aimed to be loved, honored, and obeyed— but obeyed, at any rate. Obedience he had secured, and honor had been granted him; but only now came love, the sudden love of boys for a man who was kind without being soft, who understood them well enough, but not too much, and whose private happiness linked them with their own. He began to make little jokes, the sort that schoolboys like—mnemonics and puns that raised laughs and at the same time imprinted something in the mind. There was one that never failed to please, though it was only a sample of many others. Whenever his Roman History forms came to deal with the *Lex Canuleia,* the law that permitted patricians to marry plebeians, Chips used to add: "So that, you see, if Miss Plebs wanted Mr. Patrician to marry her, and he said he couldn't, she probably replied: 'Oh yes, you can, you liar!' " Roars of laughter.

And Kathie broadened his views and opinions, also, giving him an outlook far beyond the roofs and turrets of Brookfield, so that he saw his country as something deep and gracious to which Brookfield was but one of many feeding streams. She had a cleverer brain than his, and he could not confute her ideas even if and when he disagreed with them; he remained, for instance, a Conservative in politics, despite all her radical socialist talk. But even where he did not accept, he absorbed; her young idealism worked upon his maturity to produce an amalgam very gentle and wise.

Sometimes she persuaded him completely. Brookfield, for example, ran a mission in East London, to which boys and parents contributed generously with money but rarely with personal contact. It was Katherine who suggested that a team from the mission should come up to Brookfield and play one of the School's elevens at soccer. The idea was so revolutionary that from anyone but Katherine it could not have survived its first frosty reception. To introduce a group of slum boys to the serene pleasances of better-class youngsters seemed at first a wanton stirring of all kinds of things that had better be left untouched. The whole staff was against it, and the School, if its opinion could have been taken, was probably against it too. Everyone was certain that the East End lads would be hooligans, or else that they would be made to feel uncomfortable; anyhow, there would be "incidents," and everyone would be confused and upset. Yet Katherine persisted.

"Chips," she said, "they're wrong, you know, and I'm right. I'm looking ahead to the future, they and you are looking back to the past. England isn't always going to be divided into officers and 'other ranks.' And those Poplar boys are just as important—to England—as Brookfield is. You've got to have them here, Chips. You can't satisfy your conscience by writing a check for a few guineas and keeping them at arm's length. Besides, they're proud of Brookfield—just as you are. Years hence, maybe, boys of that sort will be coming here—a few of them, at any rate. Why not? Why ever not? Chips, dear, remember this is eighteen ninety-seven—not sixty-seven, when you were up at Cambridge. You got your ideas well stuck in those days, and good ideas they were too, a lot of them. But a few—just a few, Chips—want unsticking. . . ."

Rather to her surprise, he gave way and suddenly became a keen advocate of the proposal, and the volte-face was so complete that the authorities were taken unawares and found themselves consenting to the dangerous experiment. The boys from Poplar arrived at Brookfield one

Saturday afternoon, played soccer with the School's second team, were honorably defeated by seven goals to five, and later had high tea with the School team in the Dining Hall. They then met the Head and were shown over the School, and Chips saw them off at the railway station in the evening. Everything had passed without the slightest hitch of any kind, and it was clear that the visitors were taking away with them as fine an impression as they had left behind.

They took back with them also the memory of a charming woman who had met them and talked to them; for once, years later, during the War, a private stationed at a big military camp near Brookfield called on Chips and said he had been one of that first visiting team. Chips gave him tea and chatted with him, till at length, shaking hands, the man said: "And 'ow's the missus, sir? I remember her very well."

"Do you?" Chips answered, eagerly. "Do you remember her?"

"Rather. I should think anyone would."

And Chips replied: "They don't, you know. At least, not here. Boys come and go; new faces all the time; memories don't last. Even masters don't stay forever. Since last year—when old Gribble retired—he's—um—the School butler—there hasn't been anyone here who ever saw my wife. She died, you know, less than a year after your visit. In ninety-eight."

"I'm real sorry to 'ear that, sir. There's two or three

"That was a grand day we all had—and a fine game, too."

o' my pals, anyhow, who remember 'er clear as anything, though we did only see 'er that wunst. Yes, we remember 'er, all right."

"I'm very glad. . . . That was a grand day we all had—and a fine game, too."

"One o' the best days that I ever 'ad in me life. Wish it was then and not nah—straight, I do. I'm off to Frawnce to-morrer."

A month or so later Chips heard that he had been killed at Passchendaele.

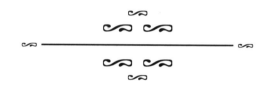

Chapter 7

*A*nd so it stood, a warm and vivid patch in his life, casting a radiance that glowed in a thousand recollections. Twilight at Mrs. Wickett's, when the School bell clanged for call-over, brought them back to him in a cloud—Katherine scampering along the stone corridors, laughing beside him at some "howler" in an essay he was marking, taking the cello part in a Mozart trio for the School concert, her creamy arm sweeping over the brown sheen of the instrument. She had been a good player and a fine musician. And Katherine furred and muffed for the December house matches, Katherine at the Garden Party that followed Speech Day Prize-giving, Katherine tendering her advice in any little problem that arose. Good advice, too—which he did not always take, but which always influenced him.

"Chips, dear, I'd let them off if I were you. After all, it's nothing very serious."

"I know. I'd like to let them off, but if I do I'm afraid they'll do it again."

"Try telling them that, frankly, and give them the chance."

"I might."

And there were other things, occasionally, that *were* serious.

"You know, Chips, having all these hundreds of boys cooped up here is really an unnatural arrangement, when you come to think about it. So that when anything does occur that oughtn't to, don't you think it's a bit unfair to come down on them as if it were their own fault for being here?"

"Don't know about that, Kathie, but I do know that for everybody's sake we have to be pretty strict about this sort of thing. One black sheep can contaminate others."

"After he himself has been contaminated to begin with. After all, that's what probably *did* happen, isn't it?"

"Maybe. We can't help it. Anyhow, I believe Brookfield is better than a lot of other schools. All the more reason to keep it so."

"But this boy, Chips . . . you're going to sack him?"

"The Head probably will, when I tell him."

"And you're going to tell the Head?"

"It's a duty, I'm afraid."

"Couldn't you think about it a bit . . . talk to the boy again . . . find out how it began. . . . After all—apart from this business—isn't he rather a nice boy?"

"Oh, he's all right."

"Then, Chips dear, don't you think there *ought* to be some other way . . ."

And so on. About once in ten times he was adamant and wouldn't be persuaded. In about half of these exceptional cases he afterward rather wished he had taken her advice. And years later, whenever he had trouble with a boy, he was always at the mercy of a softening wave of reminiscence; the boy would stand there, waiting to be told his punishment, and would see, if he were observant, the brown eyes twinkle into a shine that told him all was well. But he did not guess that at such a moment Chips was remembering something that had happened long before he was born; that Chips was thinking: Young ruffian, I'm hanged if *I* can think of any reason to let him off, but I'll bet *she* would have done!

But she had not always pleaded for leniency. On rather rare occasions she urged severity where Chips was inclined to be forgiving. "I don't like his type, Chips. He's too cocksure of himself. If he's looking for trouble I should certainly let him have it."

What a host of little incidents, all deep-buried in the past—problems that had once been urgent, arguments that had once been keen, anecdotes that were funny only because one remembered the fun. Did any emotion really matter when the last trace of it had vanished from human memory; and if that were so, what a crowd of emotions clung to him as to their last home before annihilation! He must be kind to them, must treasure them in his mind before their long sleep. That affair of Archer's resignation, for instance—a queer business, that was. And that affair about the rat that Dunster put in the organ loft while old Ogilvie was taking choir practice. Ogilvie was dead and Dunster drowned at Jutland; of others who had witnessed or heard of the incident, probably most had forgotten. And it had been like that, with other incidents, for centuries. He had a sudden vision of thousands and thousands of boys, from the age of Elizabeth onward; dynasty upon dynasty of masters; long epochs of Brookfield that had left not even a ghostly record. Who knew why the old fifth-form room was called "the Pit"? There was probably a reason, to begin with; but it had since been lost—lost like the lost books of Livy. And what happened at Brookfield when Cromwell fought at Naseby, nearby? How did Brookfield react to the great scare of the "Forty-Five"? Was there a whole holiday when news came of Waterloo? And so on, up to the earliest time that he himself could remember—1870, and Wetherby saying, by way of small talk after their first and only interview: "Looks as if we shall have to settle with the Prussians ourselves one of these fine days, eh?"

When Chips remembered things like this he often felt that he would write them down and make a book of them; and during his years at Mrs. Wickett's he sometimes went even so far as to make desultory notes in an exercise book. But he was soon brought up against difficulties— the chief one being that writing tired him, both mentally and physically. Somehow, too, his recollections lost much of their flavor when they were written down; that story about Rushton and the sack of potatoes, for instance—it would seem quite tame in print, but Lord, how funny it had been at the time! It was funny, too, to remember it; though perhaps if you didn't remember Rushton . . . and who would, anyway, after all those years? It was such a long time ago . . . Mrs. Wickett, did you ever know a fellow named Rushton? Before your time, I daresay . . . went to Burma in some government job . . . or was it Borneo? . . . Very funny fellow, Rushton. . . .

And there he was, dreaming again before the fire, dreaming of times and incidents in which he alone could take secret interest. Funny and sad, comic and tragic, they all mixed up in his mind, and someday, however hard it proved, he *would* sort them out and make a book of them. . . .

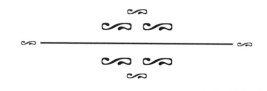

Chapter 8

*A*nd there was always in his mind that spring day in ninety-eight when he had paced through Brookfield village as in some horrifying nightmare, half struggling to escape into an outside world where the sun still shone and where everything had happened differently. Young Faulkner had met him there in the lane outside the School. "Please, sir, may I have the afternoon off? My people are coming up."

"Eh? What's that? Oh yes, yes. . . ."

"Can I miss Chapel, too, sir?"

"Yes . . . yes . . ."

"And may I go to the station to meet them?"

He nearly answered: "You can go to blazes for all I care. My wife is dead and my child is dead, and I wish I were dead myself."

Actually he nodded and stumbled on. He did not want to talk to anybody or to receive condolences; he wanted to get used to things, if he could, before facing the kind words of others. He took his fourth form as usual after call-over, setting them grammar to learn by heart while he himself stayed at his desk in a cold, continuing trance. Suddenly someone said: "Please, sir, there are a lot of letters for you."

So there were; he had been leaning his elbows on them; they were all addressed to him by name. He tore them open one after the other, but each contained nothing but a blank sheet of paper. He thought in a distant way that it was rather peculiar, but he made no comment; the incident gave hardly an impact upon his vastly greater preoccupations. Not till days afterward did he realize that it had been a piece of April foolery.

They had died on the same day, the mother and the child just born; on April 1, 1898.

Chapter 9

Chips changed his more commodious apartments in School House for his old original bachelor quarters. He thought at first he would give up his housemastership, but the Head persuaded him otherwise; and later he was glad. The work gave him something to do, filled up an emptiness in his mind and heart. He was different; everyone noticed it. Just as marriage had added something, so did bereavement; after the first stupor of grief he became suddenly the kind of man whom boys, at any rate, unhesitatingly classed as "old." It was not that he was less active; he could still knock up a half-century on the cricket field; nor was it that he had lost any interest or keenness in his work. Actually, too, his hair had been graying for years; yet now, for the first time, people seemed to notice it. He was fifty. Once, after some energetic fives, during which he had played as well as many a fellow half his age, he overheard a boy saying: "Not half bad for an old chap like him."

Chips, when he was over eighty, used to recount that

incident with many chuckles. "Old at fifty, eh? Umph—it was Naylor who said that, and Naylor can't be far short of fifty himself by now. I wonder if he still thinks that fifty's such an age? Last I heard of him, he was lawyering, and lawyers live long—look at Halsbury—umph—Chancellor at eighty-two, and died at ninety-nine. There's an—umph—age for you! Too old at fifty—why, fellows like that are too *young* at fifty. . . . I was myself . . . a mere infant. . . ."

And there was a sense in which it was true. For with the new century there settled upon Chips a mellowness that gathered all his developing mannerisms and his oft-repeated jokes into a single harmony. No longer did he have those slight and occasional disciplinary troubles, or feel diffident about his own work and worth. He found that his pride in Brookfield reflected back, giving him cause for pride in himself and his position. It was a service that gave him freedom to be supremely and completely himself. He had won, by seniority and ripeness, an uncharted no-man's-land of privilege; he had acquired the right to those gentle eccentricities that so often attack schoolmasters and parsons. He wore his gown till it was almost too tattered to hold together; and when he stood on the wooden bench by Big Hall steps to take call-over, it was with an air of mystic abandonment to ritual. He held the School List, a long sheet curling over a board; and each boy, as he passed, spoke his own name for Chips to verify and then tick off on the list. That verifying glance was an easy and favorite subject of mimicry throughout the School—steel-rimmed spectacles slipping down the nose, eyebrows lifted, one a little higher than the other, a gaze half rapt, half quizzical. And on windy days, with gown and white hair and School List fluttering in uproarious confusion, the whole thing became a comic turn sandwiched between afternoon games and the return to classes.

Some of those names, in little snatches of a chorus, recurred to him ever afterward without any effort of memory. . . . Ainsworth, Attwood, Avonmore, Babcock, Baggs, Barnard, Bassenthwaite, Battersby, Beccles, Bedford-Marshall, Bentley, Best . . .

Another one:

. . . Unsley, Vailes, Wadham, Wagstaff, Wallington, Waters Primus, Waters Secundus, Watling, Waveney, Webb . . .

And yet another that comprised, as he used to tell his fourth-form Latinists, an excellent example of a hexameter:

. . . Lancaster, Latton, Lemare, Lytton-Bosworth, MacGonigall, Mansfield . . .

Where had they all gone to, he often pondered; those threads he had once held together, how far had they scattered, some to break, others to weave into unknown patterns? The strange randomness of the world beguiled him, that randomness which never would, so long as the world lasted, give meaning to those choruses again.

And behind Brookfield, as one may glimpse a mountain behind another mountain when the mist clears, he saw the world of change and conflict; and he saw it, more than he realized, with the remembered eyes of Kathie. She had not been able to bequeath him all her mind, still less the brilliance of it; but she had left him with a calmness and a poise that accorded well with his own inward emotions. It was typical of him that he did not share the general jingo bitterness against the Boers. Not that he was a pro-Boer—he was far too traditional for that, and he disliked the kind of people who *were* pro-Boers; but still, it did cross his mind at times that the Boers were engaged in a struggle that had a curious similarity to those of certain English history-book heroes—Hereward the Wake, for instance, or Caractacus. He once tried to shock his fifth form by suggesting this, but they only thought it was one of his little jokes.

However heretical he might be about the Boers, he was orthodox about Mr. Lloyd George and the famous Budget. He did not care for either of them. And when, years later, L. G. came as the guest of honor to a Brookfield Speech Day, Chips said, on being presented to him: "Mr. Lloyd George, I am nearly old enough—umph—to remember you as a young man, and—umph—I confess that you seem to me—umph—to have improved—umph—a great deal." The Head, standing with them, was rather aghast; but L. G. laughed heartily and talked to Chips more than to anyone else during the ceremonial that followed.

"Just like Chips," was commented afterward. "He gets away with it. I suppose at that age anything you say to anybody is all right. . . ."

Chapter 10

*I*n 1900 old Meldrum, who had succeeded Wetherby as Head and had held office for three decades, died suddenly from pneumonia; and in the interval before the appointment of a successor, Chips became Acting Head of Brookfield. There was just the faintest chance that the Governors might make the appointment a permanent one; but Chips was not really disappointed when they brought in a youngster of thirty-seven, glittering with Firsts and Blues and with the kind of personality that could reduce Big Hall to silence by the mere lifting of an eyebrow. Chips was not in the running with that kind of person; he never had been and never would be, and he knew it. He was an altogether milder and less ferocious animal.

Those years before his retirement in 1913 were studded with sharply remembered pictures.

A May morning; the clang of the School bell at an unaccustomed time; everyone summoned to assemble in Big Hall. Ralston, the new Head, very pontifical and aware of himself, fixing the multitude with a cold, presaging severity. "You will all be deeply grieved to hear that His Majesty King Edward the Seventh died this morning. . . . There will be no school this afternoon, but a service will be held in the Chapel at four-thirty."

A summer morning on the railway line near Brookfield. The railway men were on strike, soldiers were driving the engines, stones had been thrown at trains. Brookfield boys were patrolling the line, thinking the whole business great fun. Chips, who was in charge, stood a little way off, talking to a man at the gate of a cottage. Young Cricklade approached. "Please, sir, what shall we do if we meet any strikers?"

"Would you like to meet one?"

"I—I don't know, sir."

God bless the boy—he talked of them as if they were queer animals out of a zoo! "Well, here you are, then— umph—you can meet Mr. Jones—he's a striker. When he's on duty he has charge of the signal box at the station. You've put your life in his hands many a time."

Afterward the story went round the School: There was Chips, talking to a striker. Talking to a striker. Might have been quite friendly, the way they were talking together.

Chips, thinking it over a good many times, always added to himself that Kathie would have approved, and would also have been amused.

Because always, whatever happened and however the

avenues of politics twisted and curved, he had faith in England, in English flesh and blood, and in Brookfield as a place whose ultimate worth depended on whether she fitted herself into the English scene with dignity and without disproportion. He had been left a vision that grew clearer with each year—of an England for which days of ease were nearly over, of a nation steering into channels where a hair's breadth of error might be catastrophic. He remembered the Diamond Jubilee; there had been a whole holiday at Brookfield, and he had taken Kathie to London to see the procession. That old and legendary lady, sitting in her carriage like some crumbling wooden doll, had symbolized impressively so many things that, like herself, were nearing an end. Was it only the century, or was it an epoch?

And then that frenzied Edwardian decade, like an electric lamp that goes brighter and whiter just before it burns itself out.

Strikes and lockouts, champagne suppers and unemployed marchers, Chinese labor, tariff reform, HMS *Dreadnought,* Marconi, Home Rule for Ireland, Doctor Crippen, suffragettes, the lines of Chatalja. . . .

An April evening, windy and rainy; the fourth form construing Vergil, not very intelligently, for there was exciting news in the papers; young Grayson, in particular, was careless and preoccupied. A quiet, nervous boy.

"Grayson, stay behind—umph—after the rest."

Then:

"Grayson, I don't want to be—umph—severe, because you are generally pretty good—umph—in your work, but today—you don't seem—umph—to have been trying at all. Is anything the matter?"

"N-no, sir."

"Well—umph—we'll say no more about it, but—umph—I shall expect better things next time."

Next morning it was noised around the School that Grayson's father had sailed on the *Titanic,* and that no news had yet come through as to his fate.

Grayson was excused lessons; for a whole day the School centred emotionally upon his anxieties. Then came news that his father had been among those rescued.

Chips shook hands with the boy. "Well—umph—I'm delighted, Grayson. A happy ending. You must be feeling pretty pleased with life."

"Y-yes, sir."

A quiet, nervous boy. And it was Grayson Senior, not Junior, with whom Chips was destined later to condole.

Chapter 11

*A*nd then the row with Ralston. Funny thing, Chips had never liked him; he was efficient, ruthless, ambitious, but not, somehow, very likable. He had, admittedly, raised the status of Brookfield as a school, and for the first time in memory there was a longish waiting list. Ralston was a live wire; a fine power transmitter, but you had to beware of him.

Chips had never bothered to beware of him; he was not attracted by the man, but he served him willingly enough and quite loyally. Or, rather, he served Brookfield. He knew that Ralston did not like him, either; but that didn't seem to matter. He felt himself sufficiently protected by age and seniority from the fate of other masters whom Ralston had failed to like.

Then suddenly, in 1908, when he had just turned sixty, came Ralston's urbane ultimatum. "Mr. Chipping, have you ever thought you would like to retire?"

Chips stared about him in that book-lined study,

startled by the question, wondering why Ralston
should have asked it. He said, at length: "No—umph—I
can't say that—umph—I have thought much about it—
umph—yet."

"Well, Mr. Chipping, the suggestion is there for you
to consider. The Governors would, of course, agree to
your being adequately pensioned."

Abruptly Chips flamed up. "But—umph—I don't
want—to retire. I don't—umph—need to consider it."

"Nevertheless, I suggest that you do."

"But—umph—I don't see—why—I should!"

"In that case, things are going to be a little difficult."

"Difficult? Why—difficult?"

And then they set to, Ralston getting cooler and harder,
Chips getting warmer and more passionate, till at last
Ralston said, icily: "Since you force me to use plain words,
Mr. Chipping, you shall have them. For some time past,
you haven't been pulling your weight here. Your methods
of teaching are slack and old-fashioned; your personal
habits are slovenly; and you ignore my instructions in a
way which, in a younger man, I should regard as rank
insubordination. It won't do, Mr. Chipping, and you must
ascribe it to my forbearance that I have put up with
it so long."

"But—" Chips began, in sheer bewilderment; and then
he took up isolated words out of that extraordinary in-
dictment. "*Slovenly*—umph—you said—?"

"Yes, look at the gown you're wearing. I happen to know

that that gown of yours is a subject of continual amusement throughout the School."

Chips knew it, too, but it had never seemed to him a very regrettable matter.

He went on: "And—you also said—umph—something about—*insubordination*—?"

"No, I didn't. I said that in a younger man I should have regarded it as that. In your case it's probably a mixture of slackness and obstinacy. This question of Latin pronunciation, for instance—I think I told you years ago that I wanted the new style used throughout the School. The other masters obeyed me; you prefer to stick to your old methods, and the result is simply chaos and inefficiency."

At last Chips had something tangible that he could tackle. "Oh, *that!*" he answered scornfully. "Well, I—umph—I admit that I don't agree with the new pronunciation. I never did. Umph—a lot of nonsense, in my opinion. Making boys say 'Kickero' at school when—umph—for the rest of their lives they'll say 'Cicero'—if they ever—umph—say it at all. And instead of 'vicissim'—God bless my soul—you'd make them say, 'We kiss 'im'! Umph—umph!" And he chuckled momentarily, forgetting that he was in Ralston's study and not in his own friendly form room.

"Well, there you are, Mr. Chipping—that's just an example of what I complain of. You hold one opinion and I hold another, and, since you decline to give way, there can't very well be any alternative. I aim to make Brook-field a thoroughly up-to-date school. I'm a science man myself, but for all that I have no objection to the classics—provided that they are taught efficiently. Because they are dead languages is no reason why they should be dealt with in a dead educational technique. I understand, Mr. Chipping, that your Latin and Greek lessons are exactly the same as they were when I began here ten years ago?"

Chips answered, slowly and with pride: "For that matter—umph—they are the same as when your predecessor—Mr. Meldrum—came here, and that—umph—was thirty-eight years ago. We began here, Mr. Meldrum and I—in—umph—in 1870. And it was—um—Mr. Meldrum's predecessor, Mr. Wetherby—who first approved my syllabus. 'You'll take the Cicero for the fourth,' he said to me. Cicero, too—not Kickero!"

"Very interesting, Mr. Chipping, but once again it proves my point—you live too much in the past, and not enough in the present and future. Times are changing, whether you realize it or not. Modern parents are beginning to demand something more for their three years' school fees than a few scraps of languages that nobody speaks. Besides, your boys don't learn even what they're supposed to learn. None of them last year got through the Lower Certificate."

And suddenly, in a torrent of thoughts too pressing to be put into words, Chips made answer to himself. These

examinations and certificates and so on—what did they
matter? And all this efficiency and up-to-dateness—what
did *that* matter, either? Ralston was trying to run Brookfield like a factory—a factory for turning out a snob cul-
ture based on money and machines. The old gentlemanly
traditions of family and broad acres were changing, as
doubtless they were bound to; but instead of widening
them to form a genuine inclusive democracy of duke and
dustman, Ralston was narrowing them upon the single
issue of a fat banking account. There never had been so
many rich men's sons at Brookfield. The Speech Day
Garden Party was like Ascot. Ralston met these wealthy
fellows in London clubs and persuaded them that Brookfield was *the* coming school, and, since they couldn't buy
their way into Eton or Harrow, they greedily swallowed
the bait. Awful fellows, some of them—though others
were decent enough. Financiers, company promoters,
pill manufacturers. One of them gave his son five pounds
a week pocket money. Vulgar . . . ostentatious . . . all
the hectic rotten-ripeness of the age. . . . And once Chips
had got into trouble because of some joke he had made
about a boy's name. The boy wrote home about it, and
his father sent an angry letter to Ralston. Touchy, no sense
of humor, no sense of proportion—that was the matter
with them, these new fellows. . . . No sense of proportion. And it was a sense of proportion, above all things,
that Brookfield ought to teach—not so much Latin or
Greek or Chemistry or Mechanics. And you couldn't ex-

pect to test that sense of proportion by setting papers and granting certificates. . . .

All this flashed through his mind in an instant of protest and indignation, but he did not say a word of it. He merely gathered his tattered gown together and with an "umph—umph" walked a few paces away. He had had enough of the argument. At the door he turned and said: "I don't—umph—intend to resign—and you can—umph—do what you like about it!"

Looking back upon that scene in the calm perspective of a quarter of a century, Chips could find it in his heart to feel a little sorry for Ralston. Particularly when, as it happened, Ralston had been in such complete ignorance of the forces he was dealing with. So, for that matter, had Chips himself. Neither had correctly estimated the toughness of Brookfield tradition, and its readiness to defend itself and its defenders. For it had so chanced that a small boy, waiting to see Ralston that morning, had been listening outside the door during the whole of the interview; he had been thrilled by it, naturally, and had told his friends. Some of these, in a surprisingly short time, had told their parents; so that very soon it was common knowledge that Ralston had insulted Chips and had demanded his resignation. The amazing result was a spontaneous outburst of sympathy and partisanship such as Chips, in his wildest dreams, had never envisaged. He found, rather to his astonishment, that Ralston was thoroughly unpopular; he was feared and respected, but not liked; and in this issue of Chips the dislike rose to a point where it conquered fear and demolished even respect. There was talk of having some kind of public riot in the School if Ralston succeeded in banishing Chips. The masters, many of them young men who agreed that Chips was hopelessly old-fashioned, rallied round him nevertheless because they hated Ralston's slave driving and saw in the old veteran a likely champion. And one day the Chairman of the Governors, Sir John Rivers, visited Brookfield, ignored Ralston, and went direct to Chips. "A fine fellow, Rivers," Chips would say, telling the story to Mrs. Wickett for the dozenth time. "Not—umph—a very brilliant boy in class. I remember he could never—umph—master his verbs. And now—umph—I see in the papers—they've made him—umph—a baronet. It just shows you—umph—it just shows you."

Sir John had said, on that morning in 1908, taking Chips by the arm as they walked round the deserted cricket pitches: "Chips, old boy, I hear you've been having the deuce of a row with Ralston. Sorry to hear about it, for your sake—but I want you to know that the Governors are with you to a man. We don't like the fellow a great deal. Very clever and all that, but a bit too clever, if you ask me. Claims to have doubled the School's endowment funds by some monkeying on the Stock Exchange. Daresay he has, but a chap like that wants watching. So if he starts chucking his weight about with you, tell him very politely he can go to the devil. The Governors don't

want you to resign. Brookfield wouldn't be the same without you, and they know it. We all know it. You can stay
here till you're a hundred if you feel like it—indeed, it's
our hope that you will."

And at that—both then and often when he recounted
it afterward—Chips broke down.

Chapter 12

So he stayed on at Brookfield, having as little to do with Ralston as possible. And in 1911 Ralston left, "to better himself"; he was offered the head-ship of one of the greater public schools. His successor was a man named Chatteris, whom Chips liked; he was even younger than Ralston had been—thirty-four. He was supposed to be very brilliant; at any rate, he was modern (Natural Sciences Tripos), friendly, and sympathetic. Recognizing in Chips a Brookfield institution, he courteously and wisely accepted the situation.

In 1913 Chips had had bronchitis and was off duty for nearly the whole of the winter term. It was that which made him decide to resign that summer, when he was sixty-five. After all, it was a good, ripe age; and Ralston's straight words had, in some ways, had an effect. He felt that it would not be fair to hang on if he could not decently do his job. Besides, he would not sever himself completely. He would take rooms across the road, with the excellent Mrs. Wickett who had once been linen-room maid; he could visit the School whenever he wanted, and could still, in a sense, remain a part of it.

At that final end-of-term dinner, in July 1913, Chips received his farewell presentations and made a speech. It was not a very long speech, but it had a good many jokes in it, and was made twice as long, perhaps, by the laughter that impeded its progress. There were several Latin quotations in it, as well as a reference to the Captain of the School, who, Chips said, had been guilty of exaggeration in speaking of his (Chips's) services to Brookfield. "But then—umph—he comes of an—umph—exaggerating family. I—um—remember—once—having to thrash his father—for it. [Laughter] I gave him one mark—umph—for a Latin translation, and he—umph—exaggerated the one into a seven! Umph—umph!" Roars of laughter and tumultuous cheers! A typical Chips remark, everyone thought.

And then he mentioned that he had been at Brookfield for forty-two years, and that he had been very happy there. "It has been my life," he said, simply. *"O mihi praeteritos referat si Jupiter annos. . . .* Umph—I need not—of course—translate. . . ." Much laughter. "I remember lots of changes at Brookfield. I remember the—um—the first bicycle. I remember when there was no gas or electric light and we used to have a member of the domestic staff called a lamp-boy—he did nothing else but clean and trim and light lamps throughout the School. I remember when there was a hard frost that lasted for

Chips received his farewell presentations and made a speech.

seven weeks in the winter term—there were no games, and the whole School learned to skate on the fens. Eighteen eighty-something, that was. I remember when two thirds of the School went down with German measles and Big Hall was turned into a hospital ward. I remember the great bonfire we had on Mafeking night. It was lit too near the pavilion and we had to send for the fire brigade to put it out. And the firemen were having their own celebrations and most of them were—um—in a regrettable condition. [Laughter] I remember Mrs. Brool, whose photograph is still in the tuck-shop; she served there until an uncle in Australia left her a lot of money. In fact, I remember so much that I often think I ought to write a book. Now what should I call it? 'Memories of Rod and Lines'—eh? [Cheers and laughter. That was a good one, people thought—one of Chips's best.] Well, well, perhaps I shall write it, someday. But I'd rather tell you about it, really. I remember . . . I remember . . . but chiefly I remember all your faces. I never forget them. I have thousands of faces in my mind—the faces of boys. If you come and see me again in years to come—as I hope you all will—I shall try to remember those older faces of yours, but it's just possible I shan't be able to— and then someday you'll see me somewhere and I shan't recognize you and you'll say to yourself, 'The old boy doesn't remember me.' [Laughter] But I *do* remember you—as you are *now*. That's the point. In my mind you never grow up at all. Never. Sometimes, for instance, when people talk to me about our respected Chairman of the Governors, I think to myself, 'Ah yes, a jolly little chap with hair that sticks up on top—and absolutely no idea whatever about the difference between a Gerund and a Gerundive.' [Loud laughter] Well, well, I mustn't go on—umph—all night. Think of me sometimes as I shall certainly think of you. *Hæc olim meminisse juvabit* . . . again I need not translate." Much laughter and shouting and prolonged cheers.

August 1913. Chips went for a cure to Wiesbaden, where he lodged at the home of the German master at Brookfield, Herr Staefel, with whom he had become friendly. Staefel was thirty years his junior, but the two men got on excellently. In September, when term began, Chips returned and took up residence at Mrs. Wickett's. He felt a great deal stronger and fitter after his holiday, and almost wished he had not retired. Nevertheless, he found plenty to do. He had all the new boys to tea. He watched all the important matches on the Brookfield ground. Once a term he dined with the Head, and once also with the masters. He took on the preparation and editing of a new Brookfeldian Directory. He accepted presidency of the Old Boys' Club and went to dinners in London. He wrote occasional articles, full of jokes and Latin quotations, for the Brookfield terminal magazine. He read his *Times* every morning—very thoroughly; and he also began to read detective stories—he had been keen on them ever since the first thrills of

Sherlock. Yes, he was quite busy, and quite happy, too.

A year later, in 1914, he again attended the end-of-term dinner. There was a lot of war talk—civil war in Ulster, and trouble between Austria and Serbia. Herr Staefel, who was leaving for Germany the next day, told Chips he thought the Balkan business wouldn't come to anything.

Chapter 13

The War years.

The first shock, and then the first optimism. The Battle of the Marne, the Russian steam-roller, Kitchener.

"Do you think it will last long, sir?"

Chips, questioned as he watched the first trial game of the season, gave quite a cheery answer. He was, like thousands of others, hopelessly wrong; but, unlike thousands of others, he did not afterward conceal the fact. "We ought to have—um—finished it—um—by Christmas. The Germans are already beaten. But why? Are you thinking of—um—joining up, Forrester?"

Joke—because Forrester was the smallest new boy Brookfield had ever had—about four feet high above his muddy football boots. (But not so much a joke, when you came to think of it afterward; for he was killed in 1918—shot down in flames over Cambrai.) But one didn't guess what lay ahead. It seemed tragically sensational when the first Old Brookfeldian was killed in action—in

September. Chips thought, when that news came: A hundred years ago boys from the School were fighting *against* the French. Strange, in a way, that the sacrifices of one generation should so cancel out those of another. He tried to express this to Blades, the Head of School House; but Blades, eighteen years old and already in training for a cadetship, only laughed. What had all that history stuff to do with it, anyhow? Just old Chips with one of his queer ideas, that's all.

1915. Armies clenched in deadlock from the sea to Switzerland. The Dardanelles. Gallipoli. Military camps springing up quite near Brookfield; soldiers using the playing fields for sports and training; swift developments of Brookfield O.T.C. Most of the younger masters gone or in uniform. Every Sunday night, in the Chapel after evening service, Chatteris read out the names of old boys killed, together with short biographies. Very moving; but Chips, in the back pew under the gallery, thought: They are only names to him; he doesn't see their faces as I do. . . .

1916. . . . The Somme Battle. Twenty-three names read out one Sunday evening.

Toward the close of that catastrophic July, Chatteris talked to Chips one afternoon at Mrs. Wickett's. He was overworked and overworried and looked very ill. "To tell you the truth, Chipping, I'm not having too easy a time here. I'm thirty-nine, you know, and unmarried, and lots of people seem to think they know what I ought to do.

Also, I happen to be diabetic, and couldn't pass the blindest M.O., but I don't see why I should pin a medical certificate on my front door."

Chips hadn't known anything about this; it was a shock to him, for he liked Chatteris.

The latter continued: "You see how it is. Ralston filled the place up with young men—all very good, of course—but now most of them have joined up and the substitutes are pretty dreadful, on the whole. They poured ink down a man's neck in prep one night last week—silly fool—got hysterical. I have to take classes myself, take prep for fools like that, work till midnight every night, and get cold-shouldered as a slacker on top of everything. I can't stand it much longer. If things don't improve next term I shall have a breakdown."

"I do sympathize with you," Chips said.

"I hoped you would. And that brings me to what I came here to ask you. Briefly, my suggestion is that— if you felt equal to it and would care to—how about coming back here for a while? You look pretty fit, and, of course, you know all the ropes. I don't mean a lot of hard work for you—you needn't take anything strenuously—just a few odd jobs here and there, as you choose. What I'd like you for more than anything else is not for the actual work you'd do—though that, naturally, would be very valuable—but for your help in other ways—in just *belonging* here. There's nobody ever been more popular than you were, and are still—

you'd help to hold things together if there were any danger of them flying to bits. And perhaps there *is* that danger. . . ."

Chips answered, breathlessly and with a holy joy in his heart: "I'll come. . . ."

Chapter 14

*H*e still kept on his rooms with Mrs. Wickett; indeed, he still lived there; but every morning, about half-past ten, he put on his coat and muffler and crossed the road to the School. He felt very fit, and the actual work was not taxing. Just a few forms in Latin and Roman History—the old lessons— even the old pronunciation. The same joke about the *Lex Canuleia*—there was a new generation that had not heard it, and he was absurdly gratified by the success it achieved. He felt a little like a music-hall favorite returning to the boards after a positively last appearance.

They all said how marvelous it was that he knew every boy's name and face so quickly. They did not guess how closely he had kept in touch from across the road.

He was a grand success altogether. In some strange way he did, and they all knew and felt it, help things. For the first time in his life he felt *necessary*—and necessary to something that was nearest his heart. There is no sublimer feeling in the world, and it was his at last.

Every morning, about half-past ten, he put on his coat and muffler and crossed the road to the School.

He made new jokes, too—about the O.T.C. and the food-rationing system and the anti–air-raid blinds that had to be fitted on all the windows. There was a mysterious kind of rissole that began to appear on the School menu on Mondays, and Chips called it *abhorrendum*—"meat to be abhorred." The story went round—heard Chips's latest?

Chatteris fell ill during the winter of seventeen, and again, for the second time in his life, Chips became Acting Head of Brookfield. Then in April Chatteris died, and the Governors asked Chips if he would carry on "for the duration." He said he would, if they would refrain from appointing him officially. From that last honor, within his reach at last, he shrank instinctively, feeling himself in so many ways unequal to it. He said to Rivers: "You see, I'm not a young man and I don't want people to—um—expect a lot from me. I'm like all these new colonels and majors you see everywhere—just a wartime fluke. A ranker—that's all I am really."

1917. 1918. Chips lived through it all. He sat in the headmaster's study every morning, handling problems, dealing with plaints and requests. Out of vast experience had emerged a kindly, gentle confidence in himself. To keep a sense of proportion, that was the main thing. So much of the world was losing it; as well keep it where it had, or ought to have, a congenial home.

On Sundays in Chapel it was he who now read out the tragic list, and sometimes it was seen and heard that he was in tears over it. Well, why not, the School said; he was an old man; they might have despised anyone else for the weakness.

One day he got a letter from Switzerland, from friends there; it was heavily censored, but conveyed some news. On the following Sunday, after the names and biographies of old boys, he paused a moment and then added:

"Those few of you who were here before the War will remember Max Staefel, the German master. He was in Germany, visiting his home, when war broke out. He was popular while he was here, and made many friends. Those who knew him will be sorry to hear that he was killed last week, on the Western Front."

He was a little pale when he sat down afterward, aware that he had done something unusual. He had consulted nobody about it, anyhow; no one else could be blamed. Later, outside the Chapel, he heard an argument:

"On the Western Front, Chips said. Does that mean he was fighting for the Germans?"

"I suppose it does."

"Seems funny, then, to read his name out with all the others. After all, he was an *enemy*."

"Oh, just one of Chips's ideas, I expect. The old boy still has 'em."

Chips, in his room again, was not displeased by the comment. Yes, he still had 'em—those ideas of dignity and generosity that were becoming increasingly rare in a frantic world. And he thought: Brookfield will take them, too, from me; but it wouldn't from anyone else.

Once, asked for his opinion of bayonet practice being carried on near the cricket pavilion, he answered, with that lazy, slightly asthmatic intonation that had been so often and so extravagantly imitated: "It seems—to me—umph—a very vulgar way of killing people."

The yarn was passed on and joyously appreciated—how Chips had told some big brass hat from the War Office that bayonet fighting was vulgar. Just like Chips. And they found an adjective for him—an adjective just beginning to be used: he was pre-War.

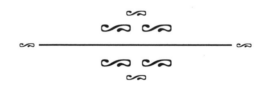

Chapter 15

And once, on a night of full moonlight, the air-raid warning was given while Chips was taking his lower fourth in Latin. The guns began almost instantly, and, as there was plenty of shrapnel falling about outside, it seemed to Chips that they might just as well stay where they were, on the ground floor of School House. It was pretty solidly built and made as good a dugout as Brookfield could offer; and as for a direct hit, well, they could not expect to survive that, wherever they were.

So he went on with his Latin, speaking a little louder amid the reverberating crashes of the guns and the shrill whine of anti-aircraft shells. Some of the boys were nervous; few were able to be attentive. He said, gently: "It may possibly seem to you, Robertson—at this particular moment in the world's history—umph—that the affairs of Cæsar in Gaul some two thousand years ago—are—umph—of somewhat secondary importance—and that—umph—the irregular conjugation of the verb *tollo*

is—umph—even less important still. But believe me—
umph—my dear Robertson—that is not really the case."
Just then there came a particularly loud explosion—quite
near. "You cannot—umph—judge the importance of
things—umph—by the noise they make. Oh dear me, no."
A little chuckle. "And these things—umph—that have
mattered—for thousands of years—are not going to be—
snuffed out—because some stink merchant—in his labo-
ratory—invents a new kind of mischief." Titters of
nervous laughter; for Buffles, the pale, lean, and medi-
cally unfit science master, was nicknamed the Stink
Merchant. Another explosion—nearer still. "Let us—
um—resume our work. If it is fate that we are soon to
be—umph—interrupted, let us be found employing ourselves in something—umph—really appropriate. Is there
anyone who will volunteer to construe?"

Maynard, chubby, dauntless, clever, and impudent, said:
"I will, sir."

"Very good. Turn to page forty and begin at the bottom line."

The explosions still continued deafeningly; the whole
building shook as if it were being lifted off its founda-
tions. Maynard found the page, which was some way
ahead, and began, shrilly:

"*Genus hoc erat pugnae*—this was the kind of fight—
quo se Germani exercuerant—in which the Germans bus-
ied themselves. Oh, sir, that's good—that's really very
funny indeed, sir—one of your very best—"

"You cannot—umph—judge the importance of things—umph— by the noise they make."

Laughing began, and Chips added: "Well—umph— you can see—now—that these dead languages—umph— can come to life again sometimes—eh? Eh?"

Afterward they learned that five bombs had fallen in and around Brookfield, the nearest of them just outside the School grounds. Nine persons had been killed.

The story was told, retold, embellished. "The dear old boy never turned a hair. Even found some old tag to il- lustrate what was going on. Something in Cæsar about the way the Germans fought. You wouldn't think there were things like that in Cæsar, would you? And the way Chips laughed . . . you know the way he *does* laugh . . . the tears all running down his face . . . never seen him laugh so much. . . ."

He was a legend.

With his old and tattered gown, his walk that was just beginning to break into a stumble, his mild eyes peering over the steel-rimmed spectacles, and his quaintly hu- morous sayings, Brookfield would not have had an atom of him different.

November 11, 1918.

News came through in the morning; a whole holiday was decreed for the School, and the kitchen staff were implored to provide as cheerful a spread as wartime rationing permitted. There was much cheering and sing- ing, and a bread fight across the Dining Hall. When Chips entered in the midst of the uproar there was an instant hush, and then wave upon wave of cheering; everyone gazed on him with eager, shining eyes, as on a symbol of victory. He walked to the dais, seeming as if he wished to speak; they made silence for him, but he shook his head after a moment, smiled, and walked away again.

It had been a damp, foggy day, and the walk across the quadrangle to the Dining Hall had given him a chill. The next day he was in bed with bronchitis, and stayed there till after Christmas. But already, on that night of November 11, after his visit to the Dining Hall, he had sent in his resignation to the Board of Governors.

When school reassembled after the holidays he was back at Mrs. Wickett's. At his own request there were no more farewells or presentations, nothing but a handshake with his successor and the word "Acting" crossed out on official stationery. The "duration" was over.

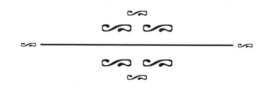

Chapter 16

And now, fifteen years after that, he could look back upon it all with a deep and sumptuous tranquillity. He was not ill, of course—only a little tired at times, and bad with his breathing during the winter months. He would not go abroad—he had once tried it, but had chanced to strike the Riviera during one of its carefully unadvertised cold spells. "I prefer—um—to get my chills—umph—in my own country," he used to say, after that. He had to take care of himself when there were east winds, but autumn and winter were not really so bad; there were warm fires, and books, and you could look forward to the summer. It was the summer that he liked best, of course; apart from the weather, which suited him, there were the continual visits of old boys. Every weekend some of them motored up to Brookfield and called at his house. Sometimes they tired him, if too many came at once; but he did not really mind; he could always rest and sleep afterward. And he enjoyed their visits—more than anything else in the world that was still to be enjoyed. "Well, Gregson—umph—I remember you—umph—always late for everything—eh—eh? Perhaps you'll be late in growing old—umph—like me—umph—eh?" And later, when he was alone again and Mrs. Wickett came in to clear away the tea things: "Mrs. Wickett, young Gregson called—umph—you remember him, do you? Tall boy with spectacles. Always late. Umph. Got a job with the—umph—League of Nations—where—I suppose— his—um—dilatoriness—won't be noticeable—eh?"

And sometimes, when the bell rang for call-over, he would go to the window and look across the road and over the School fence and see, in the distance, the thin line of boys filing past the bench. New times, new names . . . but the old ones still remained . . . Jefferson, Jennings, Jolyon, Jupp, Kingsley Primus, Kingsley Secundus, Kingsley Tertius, Kingston . . . where are you all, where have you all gone to? . . . Mrs. Wickett, bring me a cup of tea just before prep, will you, please?

The post-War decade swept through with a clatter of change and maladjustments; Chips, as he lived through it, was profoundly disappointed when he looked abroad. The Ruhr, Chanak, Corfu; there was enough to be uneasy about in the world. But near him, at Brookfield, and even, in a wider sense, in England, there was something that charmed his heart because it was old—and had survived. More and more he saw the rest of the world as a vast disarrangement for which England had sacrificed enough—and perhaps too much. But he was satisfied with Brookfield. It was rooted in things that had stood the test of time and change and war. Curious, in this deeper sense, how little it *had* changed. Boys were a politer race; bullying was nonexistent; there was more swearing and cheating. There was a more genuine friendliness between master and boy—less pomposity on the one side, less unctuousness on the other. One of the new masters, fresh from Oxford, even let the Sixth call him by his Christian name. Chips didn't hold with that; indeed, he was just a little bit shocked. "He might as well—umph—sign his terminal reports—umph—'yours affectionately'—eh—eh?" he told somebody.

During the General Strike of 1926, Brookfield boys loaded motor vans with foodstuffs. When it was all over, Chips felt stirred emotionally as he had not been since the War. Something had happened, something whose ultimate significance had yet to be reckoned. But one thing was clear: England had burned her fire in her own grate again. And when, at a Speech Day function that year, an American visitor laid stress on the vast sums that the strike had cost the country, Chips answered: "Yes, but—umph—advertisement—always *is* costly."

"Advertisement?"

"Well, wasn't it—umph—advertisement—and very fine advertisement—too? A whole week of it—umph—and not a life lost—not a shot fired! Your country would have—

umph—spilt more blood in—umph—raiding a single liquor saloon!"

Laughter . . . laughter . . . wherever he went and whatever he said, there was laughter. He had earned the reputation of being a great jester, and jests were expected of him. Whenever he rose to speak at a meeting, or even when he talked across a table, people prepared their minds and faces for the joke. They listened in a mood to be amused and it was easy to satisfy them. They laughed sometimes before he came to the point. "Old Chips was in fine form," they would say, afterward. "Marvelous the way he can always see the funny side of things. . . ."

After 1929, Chips did not leave Brookfield—even for Old Boys' dinners in London. He was afraid of chills, and late nights began to tire him too much. He came across to the School, however, on fine days; and he still kept up a wide and continual hospitality in his room. His faculties were all unimpaired, and he had no personal worries of any kind. His income was more than he needed to spend, and his small capital, invested in gilt-edged stocks, did not suffer when the slump set in. He gave a lot of money away—to people who called on him with a hard-luck story, to various School funds, and also to the Brookfield mission. In 1930 he made his will. Except for legacies to the mission and to Mrs. Wickett, he left all he had to found an open scholarship to the School.

1931. . . . 1932. . . .

"What do you think of Hoover, sir?"

"Do you think we shall ever go back to gold?"

"How d'you feel about things in general, sir? See any break in the clouds?"

"When's the tide going to turn, Chips, old boy? You ought to know, with all your experience of things."

They all asked him questions, as if he were some kind of prophet and encyclopædia combined—more even than that, for they liked their answer dished up as a joke. He would say:

"Well, Henderson, when I was—umph—a much younger man—there used to be someone who—um—promised people ninepence for fourpence. I don't know that anybody—umph—ever got it, but—umph—our present rulers seem—um—to have solved the problem how to give—umph—fourpence for ninepence."

Laughter.

Sometimes, when he was strolling about the School, small boys of the cheekier kind would ask him questions, merely for the fun of getting Chips's "latest" to retail.

"Please, sir, what about the Five-Year Plan?"

"Sir, do you think Germany wants to fight another war?"

"Have you been to the new cinema, sir? I went with my people the other day. Quite a grand affair for a small place like Brookfield. They've got a Wurlitzer."

"And what—umph—on earth—is a Wurlitzer?"

"It's an organ, sir—a cinema organ."

"Dear me. . . . I've seen the name on the hoardings,

but I always—umph—imagined—it must be some kind of—umph—sausage."

Laughter. . . . Oh, there's a new Chips joke, you fellows, a perfectly lovely one. I was gassing to the old boy about the new cinema, and . . .

Chapter 17

He sat in his front parlor at Mrs. Wickett's on a November afternoon in thirty-three. It was cold and foggy, and he dared not go out. He had not felt too well since Armistice Day; he fancied he might have caught a slight chill during the Chapel service. Merivale had been that morning for his usual fortnightly chat. "Everything all right? Feeling hearty? That's the style—keep indoors this weather—there's a lot of flu about. Wish I could have your life for a day or two."

His life . . . and what a life it had been! The whole pageant of it swung before him as he sat by the fire that afternoon. The things he had done and seen: Cambridge in the sixties; Great Gable on an August morning; Brookfield at all times and seasons throughout the years. And, for that matter, the things he had *not* done, and would never do now that he had left them too late—he had never traveled by air, for instance, and he had never been to a talkie show. So that he was both more and less experienced than the youngest new boy at the School might well be; and that, that paradox of age and youth, was what the world called progress.

Mrs. Wickett had gone out, visiting relatives in a neighboring village; she had left the tea things ready on the table, with bread and butter and extra cups laid out in case anybody called. On such a day, however, visitors were not very likely; with the fog thickening hourly outside, he would probably be alone.

But no. About a quarter to four a ring came, and Chips, answering the front door himself (which he oughtn't to have done), encountered a rather small boy wearing a Brookfield cap and an expression of anxious timidity. "Please, sir," he began, "does Mr. Chips live here?"

"Umph—you'd better come inside," Chips answered. And in his room a moment later he added: "I am—umph—the person you want. Now what can I—umph—do for you?"

"I was told you wanted me, sir."

Chips smiled. An old joke—an old leg-pull, and he, of all people, having made so many old jokes in his time, ought not to complain. And it amused him to cap their joke, as it were, with one of his own; to let them see that he could keep his end up, even yet. So he said, with eyes twinkling: "Quite right, my boy. I wanted you to take tea with me. Will you—umph—sit down by the fire? Umph—I don't think I have seen your face before. How is that?"

"I've only just come out of the sanatorium, sir—I've been there since the beginning of term with measles."

"Ah, that accounts for it."

Chips began his usual ritualistic blending of tea from the different caddies; luckily there was half a walnut cake with pink icing in the cupboard. He found out that the boy's name was Linford, that he lived in Shropshire, and that he was the first of his family at Brookfield.

"You know—umph—Linford—you'll like Brookfield— when you get used to it. It's not half such an awful place— as you imagine. You're a bit afraid of it—um, yes—eh? So was I, my dear boy—at first. But that was—um—a long time ago. Sixty-three years ago—umph—to be precise. When I—um—first went into Big Hall and—um—I saw all those boys—I tell you—I was quite scared. Indeed— umph—I don't think I've ever been so scared in my life. Not even when—umph—the Germans bombed us—during the War. But—umph—it didn't last long— the scared feeling, I mean. I soon made myself—um— at home."

"Were there a lot of other new boys that term, sir?" asked Linford shyly.

"Eh? But—God bless my soul—I wasn't a boy at all— I was a man—a young man of twenty-two! And the next time you see a young man—a new master—taking his first prep in Big Hall—umph—just think—what it feels like!"

"But if you were twenty-two then, sir—"

"Yes? Eh?"

"You must be—very old—now, sir."

Chips laughed quietly and steadily to himself. It was a good joke.

"Well—umph—I'm certainly—umph—no chicken."

He laughed quietly to himself for a long time.

Then he talked of other matters, of Shropshire, of schools and school life in general, of the news in that day's papers. "You're growing up into—umph—a very cross sort of world, Linford. Maybe it will have got over some of its—umph—crossness—by the time you're ready for it. Let's hope so—umph—at any rate. . . . Well . . ." And with a glance at the clock he delivered himself of his old familiar formula. "I'm—umph—sorry—you can't stay . . ."

At the front door he shook hands.

"Good-bye, my boy."

And the answer came, in a shrill treble: "Good-bye, Mr. Chips. . . ."

Chips sat by the fire again, with those words echoing along the corridors of his mind. "Good-bye, Mr. Chips. . . ." An old leg-pull, to make new boys think that his name was really Chips; the joke was almost traditional. He did not mind. "Good-bye, Mr. Chips. . . ." He remembered that on the eve of his wedding day Kathie had used that same phrase, mocking him gently for the seriousness he had had in those days. He thought: Nobody would call me serious today, that's very certain. . . .

Suddenly the tears began to roll down his cheeks—an

old man's failing; silly, perhaps, but he couldn't help it. He felt very tired; talking to Linford like that had quite exhausted him. But he was glad he had met Linford. Nice boy. Would do well.

Over the fog-laden air came the bell for call-over, tremulous and muffled. Chips looked at the window, graying into twilight; it was time to light up. But as soon as he began to move he felt that he couldn't; he was too tired; and, anyhow, it didn't matter. He leaned back in his chair. No chicken—eh, well—that was true enough. And it had been amusing about Linford. A neat score off the jokers who had sent the boy over. Good-bye, Mr. Chips . . . odd, though, that he should have said it just like that. . . .

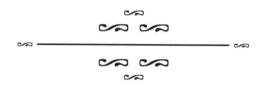

When he awoke, for he seemed to have been asleep, he found himself in bed; and Merivale was there, stooping over him and smiling. "Well, you old ruffian—feeling all right? That was a fine shock you gave us!"

Chips murmured, after a pause, and in a voice that surprised him by its weakness: "Why—um—what—what has happened?"

"Merely that you threw a faint. Mrs. Wickett came in and found you—lucky she did. You're all right now. Take it easy. Sleep again if you feel inclined."

He was glad someone had suggested such a good idea. He felt so weak that he wasn't even puzzled by the details of the business—how they had got him upstairs, what Mrs. Wickett had said, and so on. But then, suddenly, at the other side of the bed, he saw Mrs. Wickett. She was smiling. He thought: God bless my soul, what's she doing up here? And then, in the shadows behind Merivale, he saw Cartwright, the new Head (he thought

of him as "new," even though he had been at Brookfield since 1919), and old Buffles, commonly called "Roddy." Funny, the way they were all here. He felt: Anyhow, I can't be bothered to wonder why about anything. I'm going to go to sleep.

But it wasn't sleep, and it wasn't quite wakefulness, either; it was a sort of in-between state, full of dreams and faces and voices. Old scenes and old scraps of tunes: A Mozart trio that Kathie had once played in—cheers and laughter and the sound of guns—and, over it all, Brookfield bells, Brookfield bells. "So you see, if Miss Plebs wanted Mr. Patrician to marry her . . . yes, you can, you liar. . . ." Joke . . . Meat to be abhorred. . . . Joke . . . That you, Max? Yes, come in. What's the news from the Fatherland? . . . *O mihi praeteritos . . .* Ralston said I was slack and inefficient—but they couldn't manage without me. . . . *Obile heres ago fortibus es in aro.* . . . Can you translate that, any of you? . . . It's a joke. . . .

Once he heard them talking about him in the room.

Cartwright was whispering to Merivale. "Poor old chap—must have lived a lonely sort of life, all by himself."

Merivale answered: "Not always by himself. He married, you know."

"Oh, did he? I never knew about that."

"She died. It must have been—oh, quite thirty years ago. More, possibly."

"Pity. Pity he never had any children."

And at that, Chips opened his eyes as wide as he could and sought to attract their attention. It was hard for him to speak out loud, but he managed to murmur something, and they all looked round and came nearer to him.

He struggled, slowly, with his words. "What—was that—um—you were saying—about me—just now?"

Old Buffles smiled and said: "Nothing at all, old chap—nothing at all—we were just wondering when you were going to wake out of your beauty sleep."

"But—umph—I heard you—you *were* talking about me—"

"Absolutely nothing of any consequence, my dear fellow—really, I give you my word. . . ."

"I thought I heard you—one of you—saying it was a pity—umph—a pity I never had—any children . . . eh? . . . But I have, you know. . . . I have. . . ."

The others smiled without answering, and after a pause Chips began a faint and palpitating chuckle.

"Yes—umph—I have," he added, with quavering merriment. "Thousands of 'em . . . thousands of 'em . . . and all boys."

And then the chorus sang in his ears in final harmony, more grandly and sweetly than he had ever heard it before, and more comfortingly too. . . . Pettifer, Pollett, Porson, Potts, Pullman, Purvis, Pym-Wilson, Radlett, Rapson, Reade, Reaper, Reddy Primus . . . come round me now, all of you, for a last word and a joke. . . . Harper, Haslett, Hatfield, Hatherley . . . my last joke . . . did you hear it? . . . Did it make you laugh? . . . Bone, Boston, Bovey, Bradford, Bradley, Bramhall-Anderson . . . wherever you are, whatever has happened, give me this moment with you . . . this last moment . . . my boys . . .

And soon Chips was asleep.

He seemed so peaceful that they did not disturb him to say good-night; but in the morning, as the School bell sounded for breakfast, Brookfield had the news. "Brookfield will never forget his lovableness," said Cartwright, in a speech to the School. Which was absurd, because all things are forgotten in the end. But Linford, at any rate, will remember and tell the tale: "I said good-bye to Chips the night before he died. . . ."

A Note on the
Short Stories in this Volume

When *Good-bye, Mr. Chips* was published for the first time, over sixty years ago, readers around the world took the curmudgeonly schoolmaster to their hearts. Some even claimed that they had been taught by the original Mr. Chips. Such an outpouring of affection naturally delighted the author. It wasn't long before James Hilton's publisher asked him to resurrect the character, even though in *Good-bye, Mr. Chips* the schoolteacher had died peacefully in his sleep. Hilton acquiesced, creating five short stories featuring a very much alive Mr. Chips at various stages in his life. In this volume we are pleased to publish these stories in America for the first time.

—THE EDITORS

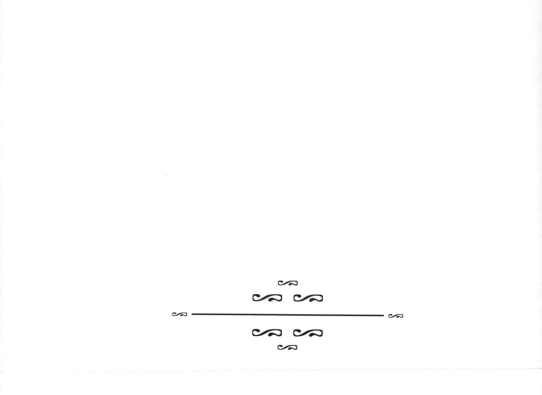

Young
Waveney

When Waveney had been at Brookfield for a month he was moved up into the lower fourth, Mr. Pearson's form; which was a pity, because he did not like Mr. Pearson. Nor, to be quite frank, did Mr. Pearson like *him*. For Waveney was everything that Mr. Pearson was not; he was young, he was attractive, and he possessed an inexhaustible vitality. Mr. Pearson, on the other hand, was no longer young; he had never been particularly attractive, and he had lately become exceedingly tired. Actually he was forty-three, and owing to a weak heart that made him ineligible for the Army, he had come to Brookfield as a wartime deputy.

How a schoolmaster must envy a boy who is obviously going to grow up into a man of much superior personality to his own, and how easily that envy can turn to loathing if the boy senses it and is cruel!

Waveney was not cruel, but he was a passionate hater of injustice, and before he had been in Mr. Pearson's class for a week, that passionate hatred was aroused.

For Mr. Pearson had a *system*. The system, which had served well enough at his previous school, was new to Brookfield; and it was as follows. If anyone in his class talked or fooled about while his back was turned, Mr. Pearson would swing round to try to catch him, but if (being rather shortsighted) he failed to do so, he would say: "Stand up, the boy who did that." Nobody would respond, of course, because there was a feeling at Brookfield that a schoolmaster had no *right* to ask such a question. He ought to spot offenders for himself, or else leave them unspotted. For after all, as young Waveney eloquently remarked, if you ride your bicycle on the footpath, you may be copped, but you aren't expected to go to the police station and give yourself up; and all life was rather like that, one way and another.

Wherefore it was manifestly unjust for Mr. Pearson, when nobody made a confession, to pull out a large gunmetal watch, hold it dramatically in one hand, and say: "Very well, if the boy who did it doesn't own up within twenty seconds, I shall detain the whole form for half an hour after morning school. . . . Five . . . Ten . . . Fifteen . . . Very well, then, you will all meet me here again at twelve-thirty."

Partly by its detestable novelty, the system worked after a few preliminary trials, and Mr. Pearson's class remained fairly free from ragging. Which, doubtless, may be held to justify the system; for Mr. Pearson knew from long experience that, in matters of class discipline, he was such stuff as screams are made of.

Now young Waveney, who was about as clever as an eleven-year-old can well be without achieving something absolutely insufferable, had declared war on Mr. Pearson right from the first day, when in answer to a question in a history test paper: "What do you know about the Star

Chamber?"—he had written: "Nothing"; and had afterward claimed full marks, because, as he said, it was a perfectly correct answer. "It wasn't *my* fault, sir, that you framed the question badly—what you *meant* to say, sir, was '*Write* what you know about the Star Chamber'—we like to be accurate about these things at Brookfield, you know, sir." Mr. Pearson did not give him full marks, but he mentally catalogued him as a boy to beware of; and Waveney mentally catalogued *him* as a poor sort of fish, anyway.

"The system," however, brought matters to a head. As Waveney urged afterward to an excited mass meeting of fourth-formers—"Can't you see that the whole thing's just beastly unfair on everybody? He can't keep order himself, and he expects us to do the job for him. If we don't own up, we're supposed to be letting other people down—sort of honor-bright business—pretty convenient for him, when you come to think about it. Well, anyhow, I warn you, I'm going to make a stand, and I advise all you others to do the same. In future, let's arrange not to own up—ever—when he tries his little game. Let him spot us himself, if he wants to—why should we save him trouble? And if he keeps us in after hours, then let's all put up with it for a time until he gets tired. He soon will. Mind now, not another confession from anybody—we'll soon break his rotten system!"

As it happened, Waveney was himself the first to make the experiment. On the following day, he threw a piece of inky paper while Mr. Pearson's back was turned, refused to confess himself the thrower when the gunmetal watch was brought out, and became thus the cause of a detention for the whole class. The detention took place, and at the end of it Mr. Pearson said: "Some coward among you has allowed you all to suffer rather than confess his own trivial misdeed. I will give him another chance to declare himself, failing which I shall have no alternative but to repeat this detention every day until Conscience has done its work."

Afterward, in rising fury, Waveney told his companions: "Well, if *that's* his game, we'll see who can stick it out the longest! Only, mind, you fellows have got to back me up! It's hard luck on you for the time being, but I'm breaking the system for you, don't forget that!"

Another detention followed on the next day, and another after that. Young Waveney became more and more tight-lipped about it; he was certainly not enjoying himself, though he was sustained by the feeling that he was leading a moral crusade. After the third detention Mr. Pearson said: "I am truly sorry for the hardship that some unspeakable coward is inflicting on you all, and if you should happen to know who he is, I don't for a moment suggest that you should tell me, but I have no doubt that you will let *him* know—in your own way—what you think of his behavior." It became disappointingly clear, moreover, that Mr. Pearson did not greatly mind the detentions; he read a novel all the time, and as he was a

*He threw a piece of inky paper while Mr. Pearson's
back was turned.*

lonely man with few social engagements an extra half-hour a day did not much matter to him.

Unfortunately the fourth form had many social engagements—in particular the annual match against Barnhurst, of which one of the detentions compelled them to miss the beginning. Ladbroke, a keen cricketer (which Waveney was not), said, rather curtly: "Pity you chose this week of all weeks for your stunt, Waveney."

After the fourth detention someone said: "Waveney daren't own up now, he's in too much of a funk—so I suppose we'll all get kept in forever."

After the fifth detention Waveney found himself suddenly unpopular, and he hated it. "Bit of a swine, young Waveney, the way he's carrying on—pity he hasn't got more guts, he'd have owned up long since. Pearson says it's a cowardly thing to do, and I reckon it is, too."

After the sixth detention Waveney went to Mr. Pearson in his room and confessed.

"Ah," said Mr. Pearson, who was not essentially an unkind man (especially when his enemy was humbled), "so you are the culprit, eh?"

"Yes."

"And it is for you that your classmates have already suffered so much—and so undeservedly?"

"Yes, I did it."

"And you found you could not go on, eh? The pangs of Conscience became too acute—the still, small voice that spoke inside you, telling you it was a mean thing to have done, a cowardly thing—isn't that what it told you, Waveney—isn't that why the tears are in your eyes?"

"No," answered Waveney, nearly howling with rage. "I think it's nothing but a dirty trap, and it's your rotten system that's really the mean and cowardly thing, and—and—"

Mr. Pearson faced Waveney with a glassy stare. His moment was spoilt. "Waveney, you forget yourself! And you will go to the Headmaster for being intolerably impudent—impudence, sir, is a thing I will *not* put up with. . . ."

So young Waveney was summoned to Chips's study that same evening. Chips was seventy then, recalled from a well-earned retirement to assume the temporary headship of Brookfield during the War years. He had been at Brookfield for nearly half a century, and he had known boys rather like young Waveney before. He had also known masters rather like Mr. Pearson before. There was not much, indeed, that Chips had not known before; only the details, the patterned configurations of events, were apt to rearrange themselves.

"Well—umph?" he said, peering over his spectacles across the desk and giving his characteristic chuckle.

"Mr. Pearson sent me, sir."

"Umph—yes—you're Waveney, yes—umph—Mr. Pearson sent me a little note about you. Some little —umph—misunderstanding—eh? Suppose you—umph— tell me about it—in your own words?"

Waveney launched into a concise account of exactly what had happened (he was really a very clear-minded boy), while Chips listened with an occasional twitching of the eyes and face. When the tale was told, Chips sat for a moment in silence, looking at Waveney. At length he said: "Bless me, boy, what a chatterer you are—you take after your father—umph—he was president of the debating society—talked the biggest—umph—nonsense— I ever heard! And now he's—umph—in Parliament—well, well, I'm not surprised. . . ."

After a pause he went on:

"But you know, Waveney—umph—you're not fair to Mr. Pearson. You'd make his life a misery—umph—if you could—and you blame him because—umph—he's found a way of stopping you! Come, come—he's got to protect himself against all you fourth-form ruffians— umph—eh?"

"But it's the system, sir."

"Systems, my boy, are hard things to fight. I warn you of that. . . . Well, I must do something with you— umph—I suppose. What do you—umph—suggest?"

"I—I don't know, sir."

"The—umph—usual?"

"If you like, sir."

"Umph—as if *I* care—so long as *you're* satisfied— umph . . . but there's one thing, Waveney. . . ."

"Yes, sir?"

"Be—be *kind,* my boy."

"*Kind,* sir?"

"Yes—umph—even when you're fighting systems. Because there are—umph—human beings—behind those systems. . . . And now—umph—run along."

Chips watched the boy's receding figure as he walked to the door across the study carpet; then, with a half-smile to himself, he called out: "Oh, Waveney—"

"Yes, sir?"

"What—umph—are you going to be when you grow up?"

"I don't know, sir."

"Well—umph—I think I can tell you. You're going to be either—umph—a great man or—umph—a confounded nuisance. . . . Or—umph—both . . . as so many of 'em are. . . . Remember that. . . . Good-bye, my boy. . . ."

After Waveney had gone, Chips sat for a time at his desk, thinking about the boy; then he wrote a note asking Mr. Pearson to come and see him.

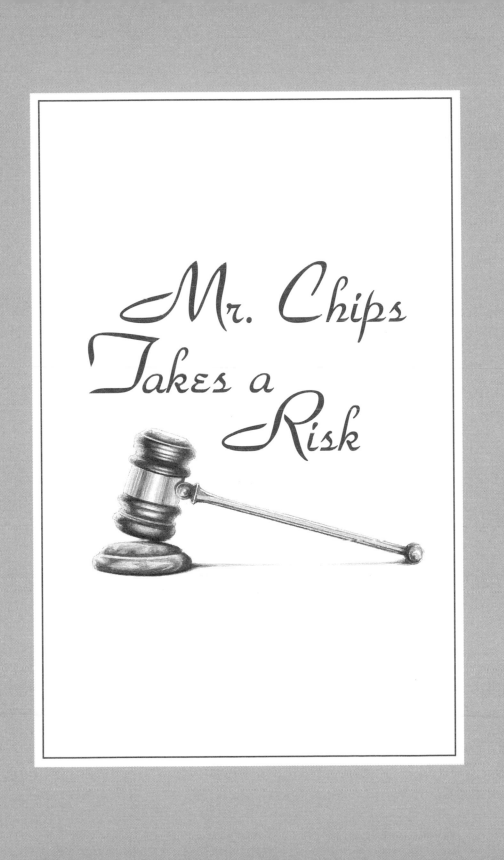

Mr. Chips Takes a Risk

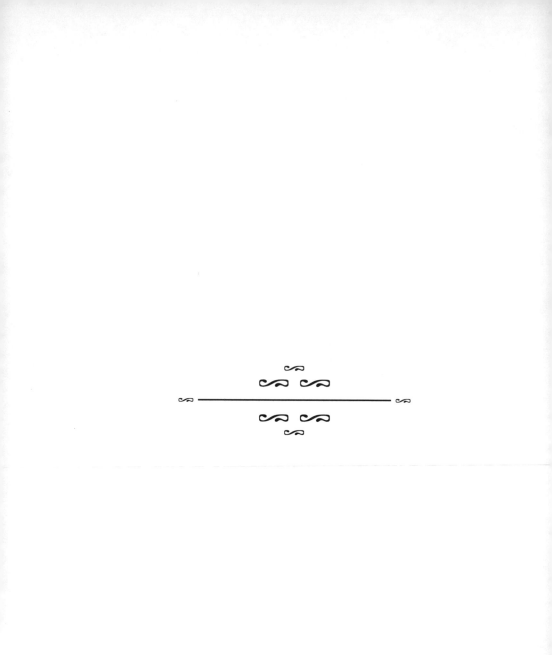

*I*t is the wise man who is often wise enough not to know too much, and in his eighty-second year Mr. Chips had grown to be very wise indeed. Living in peaceful retirement after more than half a century of schoolmastering, it was possible for him to enter his old school well aware that, in mere items of knowledge, most Brookfield boys could teach him quite as much as they could learn from him. "What *is* a straight eight?" he might ask, innocently, and when a dozen young voices had finished explaining, he would reply, with the characteristic chuckle that everyone at Brookfield had imitated for years: "Umph—umph—I see. I just wondered how an eight—umph—could possibly be straight—umph—that was all. I thought perhaps—umph—Mr. Einstein had changed—umph—even the shape of the figures. . . ."

He was always apt to joke about mathematics, partly because (as he freely confessed) he had never understood "all this—umph—$x^2 + y^2$ business." Nor, with such an attitude, was it surprising that he regarded High Finance with something of the bewilderment (but none of the adoration) with which a South Sea Islander regards a sewing machine. Indeed he once said: "Few people understand High Finance, and—umph—the higher it goes, the fewer!" He was certainly not of the few, and whenever he had any small capital to invest he put it prudently, if unadventurously, into British Government securities. Only once did he stray from this orthodox path, and that was when (on the advice of a new and excessively plausible bank manager) he bought a few shares in National and International Trust Limited, a corporation which, in the early spring of 1929, seemed as reliable as its name.

One April morning of that year Chips found the following letter on his breakfast table:

"DEAR OLD CHIPS—Just to remind you that we don't seem to have met for years. Do you remember me? You once thrashed me for climbing on the roof of the Big Hall—that was way back in 1903, which is a long time ago. If you are ever in town nowadays, do please have lunch with me at the St. Swithin's Club. I should enjoy a chat over old times.

Yours ever,
CHARLES E. MENVERS."

Which was just the sort of letter from an Old Brookfield boy that Chips delighted to receive. He replied that very morning, in his neat and very minute handwriting:

"DEAR MENVERS—Of course I remember you, and you will doubtless be glad to know that your roof exploit still holds the Brookfield record for impudence and foolhardiness. I happen to be visiting London next Thursday, so I will lunch with you then with pleasure. . . ."

So it came about that Mr. Chips entered the luxurious precincts of the St. Swithin's Club for the first time in his life and was welcomed by a handsome, fresh-complexioned man of middle age, who had once been a boy with keen eyes and a mischievous face. The eyes were still keen, and to Chips it even seemed that the look of mischief had not disappeared entirely.

"Hullo, Chips! Fine to see you again. You don't look a day older!"

They all said that. Chips answered: "I can't—umph—return the compliment. You look *many* days older!"

Menvers laughed and took the old man's arm affectionately as they entered the famous St. Swithin's dining room.

"Never been here before, Chips? Ah, well, I don't suppose business often takes you into the City. This is the Cathedral of High Finance, y'know. Why, I reckon there are a dozen millionaires having lunch in this room at the present moment. . . . And I'm one of 'em. Did you know *that?*"

No, Chips hadn't known that. "I'm afraid—umph—I never had much of a head for figures."

Menvers laughed again. There was nothing of the conventional caricatured financier about him. He was not fat, bloated, or truculent in manner. He did not wear a heavy gold watch chain—merely an inconspicuous silver wristwatch. And he did not smoke cigars—just ordinary cigarettes. Except for a veneer of self-display that was more flamboyant than really boastful, he had still the boyish charm that Chips so well remembered. And also (as he proudly confided) he had a pretty wife and one child, a boy. "Hope to put him into Brookfield in September, Chips. Keep an eye on him, won't you?"

Chips reminded him that he had long retired from schoolmastering and took no active part in the life of the modern Brookfield, but Menvers brushed the implication aside. "Nonsense, Chips. My spies report that your footsteps are heard on dark nights pacing up and down the old familiar corridors. . . . What was that tag in Vergil you used to teach us—begins *Quadrupedante putrem*—ah yes, I remember now—*Quadrupedante putrem sonitu quatit ungula campum*. Have I got it right?"

"Perfectly right," answered Chips, "except that—umph—I am not yet—umph—a ghost, and I was never—umph—a horse. . . . But I'm glad to find you still keep up your classical knowledge. It was never—umph—so considerable as to be—umph—a burden to you."

So they talked and joked together throughout a simple but exquisitely expensive meal. Chips found that he still liked Menvers, and neither more nor less because the fellow was a millionaire. Nor, in his innocence, did it occur to him as in the least remarkable that a wealthy City magnate should devote two hours of a busy day to reminiscing with an octogenarian schoolmaster. Finally, when they were on the point of shaking hands and wishing each other the best of luck, Menvers said:

"Oh, by the way, Chips, I happen to be on the board

of National and International Trust, and I saw your name on our register the other day. . . . Hardly the sort of investment for *you,* I should have thought. Quite safe, mind you—don't think there's anything wrong about it. But what's the matter with War Loan for a staid old buffer like yourself?"

Chips explained about his bank manager's recommendation, to which Menvers listened with, it seemed, a touch of exasperation. "Those fellows shouldn't take chances—why can't they leave that sort of thing to those in the game? . . . Not, mind you, that I want to give you a false impression. The stock's sound enough. . . . Fact is, I want as much of it for myself as I can get hold of. What did you pay for your packet?"

And Chips, of course, having no head for figures, couldn't remember. But by the time he reached his house at Brookfield that evening a long and (he thought) a quite unnecessarily costly telegram awaited him. It ran:

AFTER YOUR DEPARTURE I FOUND OUT PRICE YOU PAID FOR NATS AND INTERNATS STOP OFFER YOU DOUBLE IF YOU WILL SELL STOP BEG YOU TO DO SO AND DEVOTE PROFIT IF YOU WISH TO SCHOOL MISSION OR ANY SIMILAR RACKET REGARDS CHARLES THE ROOFWALKER.

Now Chips, had he been a shrewd thinker in financial matters, would have argued: This man wants my stock so urgently that he is apparently willing to pay twice the market price for it. Ergo, since he is a financier and in the know, there must be something especially promising about it, and I should do better to refuse his offer and hold on. But Chips was not a shrewd thinker of this kind. He was simple enough to feel that acceptance of the offer was an easy way of obliging Menvers and at the same time benefiting a deserving charity. So he wrote (not telegraphed) an acceptance; and that was that.

April, remember. In June, as you probably won't need to remember, National and International Trust crashed into spectacular bankruptcy. When Chips saw the newspaper headlines his immediate reaction made him write to Menvers a sympathetic note in which he said:

"I feel that your generous purchase of my shares was so recent that I cannot possibly allow you to bear any extra loss, however small, that would otherwise have fallen on me. I am therefore enclosing my check for the full amount. . . ."

By return came a scribbled postcard enclosed in an envelope:

"I have torn up your check. Don't be a damned fool. I could see this coming and I wanted to get you out in time. If you must help me, pray for me. . . ."

Two days later the arrest of Charles E. Menvers on serious and complicated charges of fraud provided the City with its biggest sensation for years.

Chips, as I have stressed all along, did not understand High Finance. His business code, so far as he had any, was simple—to sell things fairly (though in point of fact he never sold anything in his life except old books to a secondhand dealer), to pay all debts promptly (which was easy for him, as he never owed anything but gas and lighting bills), and to give generously to the needy (which was also easy for him, as he was in the habit of living well within his income). Simple—yes, simple as his life. He didn't understand the money axis on which the lives of so many people revolve—or stop revolving. What he *did* understand, however, was the notion that any one of his old boys never ceased to be *his*, no matter what happened . . . no matter *what* happened . . . and therefore, though he was old enough to find such a duty arduous, he attended every session of the four-day trial of Charles Menvers.

He sat for hours in one of the back rows of the public gallery at the Old Bailey, listening to expositions by counsel, long arguments by accounting experts, judicial rulings on incomprehensible issues, and (the only really interesting interludes) the prisoner's evidence under cross-examination. For Menvers, in that stuffy courtroom, provided the sole focus of anything even remotely aligned to humanity. The rest of the proceedings—long discussions as to the interpretation of abstruse points in company law—passed beyond Chips's intelligence as effortlessly as had the $x^2 + y^2$ of his algebra lessons seventy years before. All he gathered was that Menvers had done something (or perhaps many things) he shouldn't have done,

Menvers, in that stuffy courtroom, provided the sole focus of anything even remotely aligned to humanity.

but in a game so complicated that it must (Chips could not help feeling) be extremely difficult to know what should be done at all. Only one incident contributed much to the old man's understanding, and that was when the Crown Prosecuting Counsel asked Menvers why he had done something or other. Then had followed:

Menvers: Well, I took a chance.

C.P.C.: You mean a risk?

Menvers: A risk, if you prefer the word.

C.P.C.: And what you risked was other people's money?

Menvers: They gave it to me to risk.

C.P.C.: Why do you suppose they did that?

Menvers: Because they were greedy for the big profits that can only be obtained by taking risks, and they didn't know how to take risks themselves.

C.P.C.: I see. That is your opinion?

Menvers: Yes.

C.P.C.: You admit, then, that your policy has always been to take risks?

Menvers: Yes, always.

Chips smiled a little at that. But two hours later he did not smile when, after the verdict of "Guilty on all counts," the Judge began: "Charles Menvers, you have been found guilty of a crime which deeply stains the honor of the City of London as well as brings ruin into the lives of thousands of innocent persons who trusted you. A man of intelligence, educated at a school whose traditions you might better have absorbed, you deliberately chose to employ your gifts for the exploitation rather than for the enrichment of society. . . . It is my sad duty to sentence you to imprisonment for twelve years. . . ."

Chips paled at the words, was startled by them, could hardly believe them for a moment. And then (such was his respect for English law and its implacable impartiality) he told himself, as he shuffled out of the court: Well, I suppose it must have been something pretty serious, or they wouldn't have come down on him so hard. . . .

He had asked for permission to see Menvers during the trial, but it had not been granted; in lieu of that, he intended to offer what help he could to Mrs. Menvers, and with this object planned to intercept her as she left the court. It had not occurred to him that some scores of journalists would have the same idea, plus a greater knack in carrying it out. He did, however, contrive a meeting at her house that evening. He introduced himself and she seemed relieved to talk to him. "Twelve years!" she kept repeating. "Twelve years!"

He stayed with her for an hour, and between them, during that time, there grew a warm and gentle friendliness. "Charles was a good man," she told him, simply; and he answered: "Yes—umph—I know he was, the young rascal!"

"Young?" she echoed, and then again came the terror: "Twelve years! Oh, my God, what will he be like in twelve years?"

And Chips, touching her arm with a movement rather than a contact of sympathy, murmured: "My dear, I am eighty-one," which might have seemed irrelevant, yet was somehow the most comforting thing he could think of.

Later she said: "He's worried about the boy. We were to have sent him to Brookfield next term. Of course that's impossible now . . . the disgrace . . . everybody knowing who he is . . . that was the only thing Charles really worried about. . . ."

"Tell him not to worry," said Chips.

The next day, from Brookfield, he wrote to the prisoner in Pentonville Gaol:

"MY DEAR MENVERS—I understand that you always take risks—even on behalf of others. Take another risk, then, and send your boy to Brookfield as you had intended. . . ."

Young Menvers arrived on the first September day of the following school term, by which time his father had already served a month of the sentence. The boy was a nice-looking youngster, with more than a touch of the same eager charm that had lured thousands of profit-seekers to their doom.

On those first nights of term, despite his age and the fact that he was no longer on the official staff of the School, Chips would often take prep in substitution for some other master who had not yet arrived. He rather enjoyed being asked to do so; and the boys were equally satisfied. It relieved the misery of term-beginning to see old Chips sitting there at the desk on the platform, goggling over his spectacles, introducing new boys, and sometimes making jokes about them. Of course there was no real work done on such an evening, and it was an understood thing that one could rag the old man very gently and that he rather liked it.

But that evening there was an especial sensation—young Menvers. "I say, d'you see the fellow at the end of the third row—new boy—his name's Menvers—his father's in prison!" "No? Really?" "Yes—doing twelve years for fraud—didn't you read about it in the papers?" "Gosh, I wonder what it feels like to have your old man in quod!" "Mine said it served him right—we lost a packet through him. . . ." And so on.

And suddenly Chips, following his age-old custom, rose from his chair, his hand trembling a little as it held the typewritten sheet.

"We have—umph—quite a number of newcomers this term. . . . Umph—umph. . . . Astley . . . your uncle was here, Astley—umph—he exhibited—umph—a curious reluctance to acquire even the rudiments of a classical education . . . umph—umph. . . . Brooks Secundus. . . . These Brooks seem—umph—to have adopted the—umph—Tennysonian attribute of—umph—going on forever. . . . Dunster . . . an unfortunate name, Dunster . . . but perhaps you will claim benefit of the *lucus a non lucendo* theory . . . umph—umph . . . eh?"

Laughter . . . laughter . . . the usual laughter at the usual jokes. . . . And then, in its due alphabetical order:

"Menvers. . . ."

Chips said:

"Menvers . . . umph . . . your father was here . . . umph . . . I well remember him . . . umph . . . I hope you will be more careful than he has been—umph—lately . . . [laughter]. He was always a crazy fellow . . . and once he did the craziest thing that ever was known at Brookfield . . . climbed to the roof of the hall to rescue a kitten . . . the kitten—umph—had more sense—didn't need rescuing—so this—umph—crazy fellow—umph—in sheer petulance, I suppose—climbed to the top of the belfry—umph—and tied up the weathervane with a Brookfield tie. . . . When you go out, take a look at the belfry and think what it meant—umph—crazy fellow, your father, Menvers—umph—umph—I hope you won't take after him. . . ."

Laughter.

And afterward, alone in his sitting room across the road from the school, Chips wrote again to the prisoner in Pentonville:

"MY DEAR MENVERS—*I* took a risk too, and it was well taken. . . ."

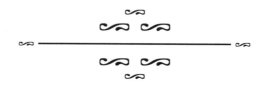

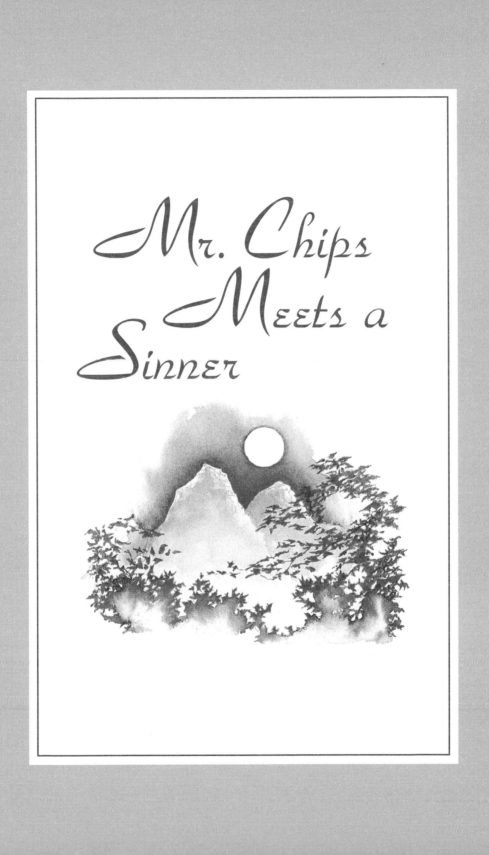

When Chips went on his annual climbing holidays he never told people he was a schoolmaster and always hoped that there was nothing in his manner or behavior that would betray him. This was not because he was ashamed of his profession (far from it); it was just a certain shyness about his own personal affairs plus a disinclination to exchange "shop" talk with other schoolmasters who might more openly reveal themselves. For when Chips was on holiday he didn't want to talk about his job—he didn't even want to think about it. Examination papers, class lists, terminal reports—all could dissolve into the thin air of the mountains, leaving not a wrack behind.

But he could never quite lose his interest in boys. And when, one September morning in 1917 in the English mountain town of Keswick, he saw an eager-faced freckled youngster of about eleven or twelve swinging astride a hotel balcony reading a book, he couldn't help intervening: "I'd be careful of that rail, if I were you. It doesn't look too safe."

The boy looked up, got up, looked down at the rail, then shook it. As if to prove Chips's point, it obligingly collapsed and set them both laughing. "So there you are," said Chips. "A minute more and you'd have been over the edge."

"Don't tell Father, that's all," answered the boy. "I'd

never hear the end of it. I once cut my head open doing the same thing. See here?" And he tilted his head as he pointed to an inch-long scar above his right temple.

"What's the book?" Chips asked, thinking it better not to admire such an obviously valued trophy.

The boy then showed the book—an anthology of poems, open at Macaulay's ballad about the coming of the Spanish Armada. "See," cried the boy, with gathering enthusiasm, "it says—'The red glare on Skiddaw roused the burglars of Carlisle.' Where's Carlisle?"

"Burghers, not burglars. Carlisle's a town about thirty miles away."

"And that's Skiddaw, isn't it?" The boy pointed to the green and lovely mountain that rose up at the back of the hotel.

"Yes, that's it."

"And who were the burglars—burghers?"

"Oh, they were just citizens of the town. When they saw the bonfires on top of Skiddaw they knew it as the signal that the Spanish Armada had been sighted."

"Oh, you know the poem, then?"

Considering that Chips had read it to his class at Brookfield for thirty years or more, he was justified in the slight smile that played over his face as he answered: "Yes, I know it."

"You like poetry?"

"Yes. Do you?"

"Yes. . . . I wish you'd come in the hotel and meet

my father. We're staying here, you know. I want to climb Skiddaw, but he says it's too much for him at his age, and he won't let me go by myself because he says I'd break my neck over a precipice."

"You probably would," said Chips, "if there *were* any precipices. But there aren't—on Skiddaw. It's a very safe mountain."

"Oh, do come along and tell him that. . . ."

So Chips, almost before he realized what was happening, found himself piloted inside the breakfast room and presented to Mr. Richard Renshaw, a squat, pasty-faced, pompous-mannered heavyweight of fifty or thereabouts. One glance at him was enough to explain his reluctance to climb Skiddaw, and one moment of his conversation was enough to suggest that the boy's love of poetry would awake no answering sympathy in the father. "I'm a plain man," began Mr. Renshaw, expounding himself with great vigor in a strong Lancashire accent. "Just an ordinary plain businessman—I don't claim to be anything else. I'm here because my doctor said I needed a rest cure—and there's no rest cure to me in pushing myself up the side of a mountain. So David must just stay down with me and make the best of it. Especially as it's due to him— very largely—that I *need* the rest cure."

He glanced at the boy severely, but the latter made no comment and showed no embarrassment. Presently David moved away and left the two men together.

"That boy's a terror," continued Mr. Renshaw, pointing after him.

"He's not mine, understand—he's my second wife's by an earlier marriage. *My* lad's quite different—fine young chap of twenty-five—accountant in Birmingham—settled down very nicely, *he* has. But David . . . well, it's my belief there's bad blood in him somewhere."

Chips went on listening—there was nothing else to do.

"Been sacked from two schools already . . . a proper good-for-nothing, if you ask me."

Chips hadn't asked him, but now he did ask, with the beginnings of interest: "What was he sacked for?"

"Well, from the first school it was for breaking into the matron's bedroom in the middle of the night and scaring her out of her wits . . . and the second school sacked him for an outrageous piece of hooliganism in the school chapel during Sunday service. Isn't that enough?"

"Quite enough," agreed Chips. "But what's the position now? What are you going to do with him?"

"I'm damned if I know. What can *anybody* do with him? If schoolmasters themselves . . . but it's my belief they don't try. I've not a lot of faith in schoolmasters."

"Neither have I—sometimes," said Chips.

During the days that followed, Chips would have had more and better chances to get to know David if Mr. Renshaw himself had been less obtrusive. He seemed a lonely, unhappy sort of man, and, having found in Chips a tolerant listener, he made the most of his opportunitics. Chips could hardly get rid of the fellow at the hotel, and was heartily glad that he was no mountaineer. It was not that there was anything especially unpleasant about him—merely that he was a loud-voiced nuisance, and the more Chips saw and talked with him the more he felt that David, with or without bad blood, could not have found life very harmonious with such a stepfather. Chips wondered why such an ill-assorted pair chose to take their holidays together. The answer came in Renshaw's own words. "Y'see, Chipping, there's nowhere else for him to go. The rest of the family wouldn't take him as a gift—and you can't blame 'em. So he has to stay with me whether he likes it or not. I'm here for my health and he's here for his sins."

Chips smiled. "I only hope my own sins will never take me to a worse place."

"Oh, Keswick's all right, I know. Quite a nice spot for a holiday. But the boy isn't satisfied with a stroll in the afternoon—he's restless all the time—restless as a monkey. Only the other day one of the waiters caught him in the hotel kitchen tasting all the food out of the pans . . . of course I had to give the fellow a tip to say nothing about it. The boy's incorrigible, I tell you. Hasn't even the sense to see what's to his own advantage. He knows that his whole future depends on what I decide to do with him during the next few days."

"Oh?"

"Well, y'see, I promised that if he was a good boy I'd

overlook his disgraceful behavior at school and put him under a private tutor for a couple of years—then after that, if he still behaved well, my son in Birmingham— the accountant, y'know—might take him into his office. . . . Wonderful chance, that, for a boy who's had to leave school under a cloud. . . . You'd think it would make him turn over a new leaf, wouldn't you? But it doesn't . . . he doesn't seem to care."

Which was true enough. David's efforts to impress his stepfather with any appearance of remorse or future good intentions were, Chips could see, so vagrant as to be almost imperceptible. Once Chips gave the boy a lead to discuss the matter by saying, during a casual conversation in the hotel lobby: "By the way, your father says there's a chance of your becoming an accountant. . . . It's a good profession, if you like it."

"I wouldn't like it," answered David, with decision.

"What do you want to be, then?"

"An explorer."

Chips smiled. "That's not a very easy thing to be, nowadays."

"I once explored some caves in Scotland. It was easy enough. It was Father who made all the fuss about it."

"Oh?"

"Just because the tide came up and I had to sit on a ledge all night and wait for it to go down again. But I didn't find any gems."

"Any gems? What do you mean?"

"Well, it said in the poem, you know—'Full many a gem of purest ray serene the dark unfathomed caves of ocean bear.' . . . But I didn't find any."

Toward mid-September, as the beginning of term at Brookfield approached, Chips began to feel the familiar willingness to be back at work. His strenuous month of walking and climbing had made him feel immensely fit for his years; even Renshaw's conversations couldn't spoil such a holiday, despite their tendency to become less restrained and more repetitive. They dealt largely with the trials and tribulations of family and business life; Renshaw had not been a happy man, nor—quite evidently—had he possessed the knack of making others happy. It seemed that he had lost a great deal of money owing to the War. He couldn't forget it, and Chips, for whom money meant little and for whom the War (then in its third year) was a continuing nightmare, was scarcely interested to hear in great detail how certain properties of his in Germany had been confiscated. "There never was anything like it," said Renshaw, mournfully philosophizing. "And I'd put so much into them. That's what the War does."

Chips could have told him of other and perhaps worse things that the War did, but he refrained.

"And it's nearly as bad over here, Chipping, the way the export trade's going to pieces," Renshaw continued. "I'm in cotton, and I know." And he added, putting the direct question: "What are you in?"

"I'm in clover," answered Chips, almost to himself.

Renshaw looked puzzled. "What's that? . . . Oh, I see—I suppose you mean you sold out in time and can sit back on the profits? . . . Lucky fellow—I wish *I* had."

"Yes, I think I've been pretty lucky," agreed Chips, leading the conversation gently astray.

There came the last evening. Both Chips and the Renshaws were to leave the following morning—in different directions, Chips was not sorry to realize. As a kindly gesture toward someone whom he did not definitely dislike (though he was aware that they had little in common), he agreed to visit Renshaw's room after dinner for a final drink and chat. He did this dutifully, listening in patience to the man's renewed plaints against the state of trade and affairs in general; about ten o'clock he thought he could decently take his leave. "I don't suppose we'll meet in the morning," he said. "I'd like to have said good-bye to David, but I suppose he's in bed by now."

"Not he," answered Renshaw. "I packed him off to the pictures to keep him out of the way while we had our talk. There's Chaplin on or something. . . . He can't get into much mischief in a cinema. Ought to be back any minute now."

"Well, say good-bye to him for me," said Chips, shaking hands.

But about midnight he was awakened by a tapping at his room door. Renshaw, in nightshirt and dressing gown, stood outside. "I say, Chipping . . . sorry to wake you up . . . but David hasn't come back yet. What do you suppose I ought to do about it? Call the police?"

They adjourned to Renshaw's room to discuss the situation further. It was a night of bright moonlight and Chips, standing by the window, could see the full curve of Skiddaw outlined against a blue-black sky. He thought he had never seen the mountain look more beautiful, and he remembered, with a sharp ache of longing, his first meeting with his wife on another mountain not many miles away—the lovely girl whose marriage and death had taken place twenty years before, yet whose memory still lay as fresh as moonlight in his heart. And he knew, in some ways, that it was David as well as the mountain that had made him think of her, for she would have liked David, would have known how to deal with him—she had always known how to deal with boys, and whatever he himself had learned of that difficult art, the most had been from her.

He said quietly: "I'd give him a bit more time before calling the police, if I were you. After all, it's a nice night— he may have gone for a walk."

"Gone for a walk? At midnight? Are you crazy?"

"No . . . but *he* may be . . . a little. . . . In fact . . ." And then suddenly Chips, turning his eyes to the mountain again, saw at the very tip of the summit a strange phenomenon—a faintly pinkish glow that might almost have been imagined, yet—on the other hand—might almost not have been. "Yes," he added, "I think he *is* a little crazy. . . . Do you mind if I go out and look for him? . . . I have an idea . . . well, let me look for him, anyway. And you wait here . . . don't call for help . . . till I come back. . . ."

Chips dressed and hurriedly left the hotel, walked through the deserted streets, and then, at the edge of the town, turned to the sidetrack that led steeply up the flank of the mountain. He knew his way; the night was brilliant; he had climbed Skiddaw many times before. A certain eagerness of heart, a feeling almost of youth, infected him as he climbed—an eagerness to find out if his guess were true, and a gladness to find that he could still climb a three-thousand-foot mountain without utter exhaustion. He clambered on, till at last the town lay beneath in spectral panorama, its roofs like pebbles in a silver pool. Life was strange and mysterious, nearer perhaps to the heart of a boy than to the account books of a man. . . . And presently, reaching the rounded hump that was the summit, Chips heard a voice, a weak, rather scared, treble voice that cried: "Hello—hello!"

"Hello, David," said Chips. "What are you doing up here?"

(Quite naturally, without excitement or indignation, just as if it were the most reasonable thing in the world for a boy to be on top of Skiddaw at two in the morning.)

"I've been trying to make a bonfire," David replied,

"I've been trying to make a bonfire. . . . I wanted to rouse the burglars of Carlisle."

sadly. "I wanted to rouse the burglars of Carlisle. But the wind kept blowing it out . . . and I'm tired and cold. . . ."

"You'd better come down with me," said Chips, taking the boy's arm. A few half-burned newspapers at their feet testified to the attempt that had been made. "And you needn't worry about the burghers of Carlisle—burghers, not burglars—they're all fat, elderly gentlemen who're so fast asleep at this time of night that they wouldn't see anything even if you'd set the whole mountain on fire. . . . So come on down."

David laughed. "Are burghers like that? They sound like Father."

"Oh no. He's anything but fast asleep. He's worried about where you've got to."

"Don't tell him you found me up here. Please don't tell him. Say I just went for a walk and got lost and you found me."

"Why don't you want me to tell him the truth?"

"He wouldn't understand. . . ."

"And do you think *I* do?"

"I don't know. Somehow . . . I think you do in a way. . . . There's something about you that makes it easy for me to tell you things. . . . Do you know what I mean?"

On the way down the mountain Chips talked to David quite a lot, and David, thus encouraged, gave his own versions of the escapades that had led to his expulsion from two schools.

"You see, Mr. Chipping . . . it was a line from one of

Browning's poems—I'm like that about poetry, you
know—a line gets hold of me sometimes—I can't help
it . . . sort of makes me do things—crazy things. . . .
Well, anyway, this was a line about trees bent by the
wind over the edge of a lake . . . it said they bent over
'as wild men watch a sleeping girl.' . . . I just couldn't
forget that, somehow . . . it thrilled me . . . I wanted
to act being a wild man . . . but I didn't know any sleeping girl . . . so I dressed up in a blanket and blacked my
face and climbed in through the matron's window . . .
of course, she wasn't exactly a girl, but she was asleep,
anyway. . . . Oh, she was asleep all right . . . but she
woke up while I was watching her . . . and my goodness, how she screamed."

"And that's what you were expelled for?"

"Yes."

"I suppose she didn't believe your explanation?"

"Nobody did."

"Well . . . tell me about the other school. . . . What
did they expel you for there?"

"Oh, that was different. . . . You see, there was a
preacher who used to visit us regularly and he always
used to pray something about the weather—if there was
a drought he'd pray for rain, and if there were floods he'd
pray for the rain to stop, and so on. Seemed to me he
just did it as a matter of course—so I thought it would
be fun to find out if he'd really be surprised to have a
prayer answered right away. . . . There was a sort of

trapdoor in the chapel roof just over the pulpit, and one Sunday during the summer term, after there'd been no rain for a month, I guessed he'd start praying for it, and he did . . . so I just opened the trapdoor and tippled a bucket of water over him. . . . I thought he might think I was God. . . ."

When Chips and David reached the hotel, the first glimmer of dawn lay over the mountain horizon. Renshaw was pacing up and down in his room, perplexed, alarmed, and—as soon as he saw David—in a furious rage. Chips tried, and eventually was able, to pacify him somewhat. They all breakfasted together a few hours later—David, very tired and subdued, half dozing over ham and eggs. Renshaw was still—and perhaps not without reason—in a grumbling mood.

"I'm damned if I know *what* to do with him," he said, glancing distastefully at his stepson, and careless whether the boy heard his words or not. "If only schoolmasters were any use I'd try to send him to another place, but they won't have him, y'know, when they find out he's been sacked twice already. Damned lazy fellows, schoolmasters—take your money and then say the job's too hard for them. After all, that's what they're paid for, to deal with boys—even with bad boys—why do they shirk it? . . . I tell you, I've no patience with schoolmasters—too easy a life, too many holidays—they don't know what real work is. . . . What's your opinion, Chipping?"

Chips smiled. "Perhaps it's a prejudiced one, Mr. Renshaw," he answered. "You see, I *am* a schoolmaster."

"*What?* Oh . . . I didn't mean . . ."

"Don't apologize—I'm not offended. . . . I should never have told you except that . . . well, I wonder if you'd consider sending David to Brookfield . . . he could be—umph—directly under my—I won't say 'control'— let's call it 'guidance.' . . ."

"Do you really mean it?"

"Yes."

"Well, I'm sure it's very generous of you. . . ."

"Not at all. It's just that—as you say—schoolmasters oughtn't to shirk their jobs."

At this point David looked up from his dozing and Renshaw turned to him. "David—did you hear that? Mr. Chipping is a schoolmaster . . . how would you like to go to his school?"

David stared at Chips and Chips looked at David and they both began to smile. Then David said: "*What?* You a schoolmaster? I don't believe it!"

"I take that as a compliment," answered Chips.

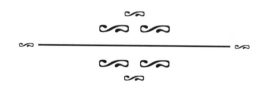

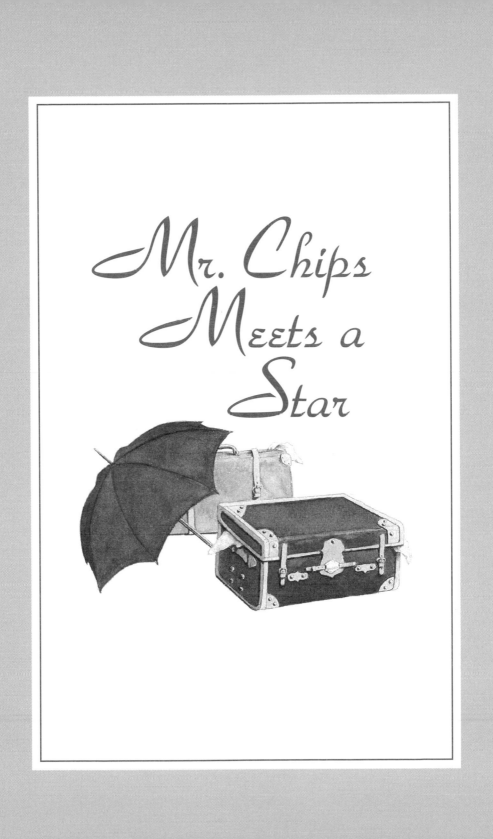

Mr. Chips Meets a Star

*C*oming out of the Royal Hotel the other day, who should I espy but Randolph Renny . . ." wrote Miss Lydia Jones ambiguously, ungrammatically, but in substance correctly. For it really was Randolph Renny himself, and by identifying him she made the scoop of a lifetime. A pretty long lifetime, too, for she had been doing an unpaid-for social gossip column for the *Brookfield Gazette* for over thirty years. Prim and spinsterish, she knew the exact difference (if any) between a pianoforte solo "tastefully rendered" and one "brilliantly performed"; and three times a year, at the Brookfield School end-of-term concert, she sat in the front row, notebook and pencil in hand, fully aware of herself as Brookfield's critical and social arbiter.

She had occupied this position so long that only one person could clearly remember her as an eager, ambitious girl, hopeful about her first and never-published novel; and that person was Chips. She had been a friend of his wife's, which was something he could never forget. As she grew primmer and more spinsterish with the years, he sometimes meditated on the strange chemistry of the sexes that so often enabled a man to ripen with age where a woman must only wither; and when she withered out of her fifties into her sixties, and Brookfield began to laugh at her and the *Gazette* to print fewer and fewer of her contributions, then Chips's attitude became even more gentle and benevolent. Poor old thing—she meant no harm, and she loved her work. He would always stop for a chat if he met her in the village, and he only smiled when, from time to time, she referred to him as "the doyan [*sic*] of the Brookfield staff."

Indeed, it was Chips who had given her the scoop about Randolph Renny—a scoop which many a bright young man from Fleet Street would have paid good money for. But Chips chose to give it to Miss Lydia Jones, of the *Brookfield Gazette,* and Miss Jones, faced with something far outside her customary world of whist drives and village concerts, could only deal with it in the way she dealt with most things . . . that is to say, ambiguously, ungrammatically, but in substance correctly.

This is how it had all happened. One August evening Chips had been returning by train from London to Brookfield. The School was on summer vacation, and though he had long since retired from active teaching work (he was over eighty), he still experienced, during vacations, a sense of being on holiday himself. Traveling back after an enjoyable weekend with friends, he had been somewhat startled by the invasion of his compartment at the last moment by a youngish, almost excessively handsome, and certainly excessively well-dressed fellow, who slumped down into a corner seat breathlessly, mopped his forehead with a silk handkerchief, and absurdly overtipped a porter who threw in

*It was Chips who had given her the scoop
about Randolph Renny.*

after him some items of very rich and strange luggage.

Now it was Chips's boast that he never forgot the faces of his old boys, that somehow their growing up into manhood made no difference to his powers of recognition. That was mainly true; but as he grew older he was apt to err in the other direction, to recognize too often, to accost a stranger by name and receive the bewildered reply that there must be some mistake, the stranger had never been to Brookfield School, had never even heard of Brookfield, and so on. And on such occasions, a little sad and perhaps also a little bothered, Chips would mumble an apology and wonder why it was that his memory could see so much more clearly than his eyes.

And now, in the train, memory tempted him again— this time with the vision of a good-looking twelve-year-old who had almost established a record for the minimum amount of Latin learnable during a year in Chips's classical form. So he leaned forward after a few moments and said to the still breathless intruder: "Well—umph— Renny . . . how are you?"

The young man looked up with a rather scared expression. "I beg you, sir, not to give me away . . ." he stammered.

"Give you away . . . umph . . ." Some joke, obviously— Renny had always been one for jokes. "What is it you've been up to this time—umph?"

"I'm trying to get away from the crowd—I thought I'd actually succeeded. . . . I chose this compartment because—if you'll pardon me for saying it—I noticed you were reading the paper through double spectacles—so I guessed—I hoped—"

"I may be—umph—a little shortsighted, Renny— but I assure you—umph—I never forget a Brookfield face. . . ."

"Brookfield? Why, that's where I'm going to. What sort of a place is it?"

Chips looked astonished. Surely this was carrying a joke too far. "Much the same—umph—as when you were there fifteen years ago, my boy."

Then the young man looked astonished. "I? . . . But— but I've never been there before in my life—this is my first visit to England, even. . . . I don't understand."

Neither did Chips understand, though he certainly— now that the other had suggested it—detected an accent from across the sea. He said: "But—your name—it's Charles Renny . . . isn't it?"

"Renny, yes, but not Charles . . . Randolph—that's my name—Randolph Renny. I thought you recognized me."

"I thought so, too. I—umph—must apologize."

"Well, I hope you won't give me away now that I've told you."

"Give you away? I—umph—I don't know what you're driving at."

"My being Randolph Renny—that's what I mean. I'm traveling incognito."

"Mr. Renny, I'm afraid I still don't understand."

"You mean you don't recognize my name?"

"I fear not. . . . My own name—since you have been good enough to introduce yourself—is Chipping."

"Well, Mr. Chipping . . . you fairly beat the band. I reckon you must be the only person on this train who hasn't seen one or other of my pictures."

"Pictures? You are an artist?"

"I should hope so. . . . Oh, I get you—you mean a painter? . . . No, not that sort of artist. I'm on the films. Don't you ever go to the cinema?"

Chips paused; then he answered, contemplatively: "I went on one occasion only—umph—and that was ten years ago. I am given to understand—umph—that there have been certain improvements since then . . . but the—umph—poster-advertising outside has never—umph—tempted me to discover how far that is true."

Renny laughed. "So that's why you've never heard my name? My goodness, wouldn't I like to show you round Hollywood! . . . I suppose you're not interested in acting?"

"Indeed, yes. In my young days I was a great admirer of Henry Irving and Forbes-Robertson and—umph—Sarah Bernhardt—and the immortal Duse—"

"I guess none of them ever got three thousand fan letters a week—as I do."

"*Fan* letters?"

"Letters from admirers—total strangers—all over the world—who write to me."

Chips was bewildered. "You mean—umph—you have to read three thousand letters a week?"

"Well, I don't read 'em. But my secretary counts 'em."

"Dear me—umph—how extraordinary. . . ." And after a little pause for thought, Chips added: "You know, Mr. Renny, I feel—umph—somewhat in the mood of the late Lord Balfour when he was taken to see the sights of New York. He was shown the—umph—I think it is called the Woolworth Building—and when—umph—the boast was made to him that it was completely fireproof, all he could reply was—'What a pity!' "

"Good yarn—I must remember it. Tell me something about this place Brookfield."

"It's just a small English village. A pleasant place, I have always thought."

"You know it well?"

"Yes, I think I can say I do. . . . But why—if I may ask—are you going there?"

"Darned if I know myself, really. Matter of fact, it's my publicity man's idea, not mine. Fellow named McElvie—smart man. . . . You see, Mr. Chipping, your English public—bless their hearts—have fussed over me so much during the last few weeks that I'm all in—gets on your nerves after a time—signing autographs and being mobbed everywhere . . . so I said to McElvie, I'm going to take a real rest cure, get away to some little place and hide myself, travel incognito . . . just some little place in the country—must be lots of places like that in

England . . . and then McElvie suddenly had one of his bright ideas. You see, I was born in Brooklyn, so he looks it up and finds there isn't a Brooklyn in England, but there's a Brookfield. Sort of sentimental association . . . you see?"

"I see," answered Chips, without seeing at all.

He could not really understand why a man born in Brooklyn should have a sentimental desire to visit Brookfield: He could not understand why letters should be counted instead of read; he could not understand why a man who wished to avoid publicity should travel around with the kind of luggage that would rivet the attention of every fellow traveler and railway porter. These things were mysteries. But he said, with a final attempt to discover what manner of man this Randolph Renny might be: "In my young days we used—umph—to classify actors into two kinds—tragedians and comedians. Which kind are you, Mr. Renny?"

"I guess I'm not particularly either. Just an actor."

"But—umph—for what parts did you become—umph—famous?"

"Oh, heroes, you know—romantic heroes. Fact is . . . I guess it sounds stupid, but I can't help it. . . . I've sometimes been labeled the world's greatest lover."

Chips raised his eyebrows and answered: "I have a good memory for faces—umph—and also for names—umph—but in the circumstances, Mr. Renny, it seems fortunate that I—umph—easily forget reputations. . . ."

Thus they talked till the train arrived at Brookfield, by which time Chips had grown rather to like the elegant strange young man who seemed to have acquired the most fantastic renown by means of the most fantastic behavior. For Chips, listening to Renny's descriptions of Hollywood life, could not liken it to anything he had ever experienced or read about. For instance, Renny had a son, and in Hollywood, so he said, the boy was taken to and from school every day in a limousine accompanied by an armed bodyguard—the reason being that Renny had received threatening letters from kidnappers. "To tell you the truth, Mr. Chipping, I almost thought of sending him to a school in England. D'you know of any good school?"

"Umph," replied Chips, thinking the matter over—or rather, not needing to think the matter over. "There is a school at Brookfield."

"A good school?"

"Well, I have—umph—some reason—to believe so."

"You were educated there yourself?"

Chips answered, with a slow chuckle: "Yes . . . umph. . . . I rather imagine I have picked up a little knowledge there during—umph—the past half-century or so. . . ."

By such exchanges of question and answer Chips and Hollywood's ace film star came to know each other and each to marvel at the strange world that the other inhabited. It was on Chips's advice that Renny tore some of the labels off his luggage and wrapped up his Fifth Avenue hatbox in brown paper and did a few other simple things to frustrate the publicity he was apparently fleeing from. And at the Royal Hotel (still taking Chips's advice) he registered as plain Mr. Read, of London, and was careful to ask for "tomahtoes," not "tomaitoes," and to refrain from asking for ice water at all. A few days later he rang up Chips on the telephone, said he was feeling a little bored, and suggested a further meeting. Chips asked him to tea at his rooms opposite the School, and afterward showed him over the School buildings. Renny was horrified at the primitiveness of the School bathrooms, and was still more horrified when Chips told him they had just been modernized. But he was pleased and relieved when Chips told him that there had not been a single case of kidnapping at Brookfield for the past three hundred years. "Before that—umph—I cannot definitely say," added Chips. "There were very disturbed times— we had a headmaster hanged during the sixteenth century for preaching the wrong kind of sermon— yes—umph—we have had disturbed times, Mr. Renny."

"You talk about them, sir, as if they were only yesterday."

"So they were," replied Chips, "in the history of England. And Brookfield is a part of that."

"And you're a part of Brookfield, I guess?"

"I should like to think so," answered Chips, pouring himself tea.

The two men met again, several times. One afternoon they lazed in deck chairs on the deserted School playing fields; another day Chips took Renny to the local parish church, showed him the points of historic interest in it, and introduced him to the verger and the vicar as a visiting American. Renny seemed surprised that neither recognized him, and uttered a word of warning afterward, "You know, Mr. Chipping, you're taking a big chance showing me round like that."

"No," replied Chips. "I think not. There are—umph—quite a number of people in England who—umph—have never heard of you, Mr. Renny. The vicar here, for instance, is much more familiar with the personalities of Rome during the age of Diocletian—he has written several books on the subject . . . while our verger is so passionately devoted to the cultivation of roses that—umph—I doubt if he ever goes to the cinema at all. . . . So I think you may feel quite safe in Brookfield—nobody will annoy or molest you."

But after another few days had passed and there had been other meetings, a dark suspicion began to enter Chips's mind. Renny looked much better for his rest cure; idle days in sunshine and fresh air had soothed the tired nerves of an idol whose pedestal too often revealed him as merely a target. All the same, there was this dark suspicion—a suspicion that suggested itself most markedly whenever the two men walked about the streets of Brookfield. Just this—that though Renny was doubtless sincere in wanting to get away from crowds of autograph-hunting admirers, he did not altogether relish the ease with which in Brookfield he was doing so. There were moments when, perhaps, the success of his incognito peeved him just a trifle. It would have been truly awful if a mob of girls had torn the clothes off his back (they had done this several times in America), but when they didn't, then . . . well, there were moments when Renny's attitude might almost have been diagnosed as: Why the hell don't they try to, anyway? . . .

All of which came to a head in the sudden appearance of McElvie on the scene. This wiry little Scots-American arrived in Brookfield like a human tornado, expressed himself delighted with the improvement in Renny's health, demanded to meet the old gentleman with whom he had been spending so much time, wrung Chips's hand effusively, and opined (gazing across the road at the School buildings) that it certainly looked "a swell joint."

"And see," he added, taking Renny and Chips by the arm and drawing them affectionately together, "I've got a swell idea, too. . . . I'll work up a lot of phooey in the papers about your disappearance. . . . 'Where is Randolph Renny?'—'Has anybody seen him?'—'He's hiding somewhere—where is it?'—you know the sort of thing . . . and then, when all the excitement's just boiling over, we'll discover you here . . . spending a vacation with the old professor. . . ."

"I'm not a professor . . ." protested Chips, feebly.

"Aw, it's the same thing . . . and you knew Irving, too . . . and Forbes-Robertson . . . Sarah Bernhardt . . . the immortal Dewser. . . ."

"I didn't know them," protested Chips, still feebly. "I only saw them act."

"Aw, what does that matter? . . . after all, you saw 'em and you're old enough to have known the whole bunch of 'em . . . they gave you tips about acting—and you took in what they said—and now you pass it all on to Renny here. . . . Oh, boy, what an idea—handing on the great tradition—Randolph Renny vacations secretly with Dewser's oldest friend—you were roommates, maybe, you and Dewser—"

"Hardly," answered Chips. "It was—umph—before the days of co-education. . . ."

"Oh, a woman?" replied McElvie, seizing the point with an alertness Chips could not but recognize and admire. "I beg your pardon, Mr. Chipping—no offense meant, I'm sure. . . . But you got the idea, haven't you?— why it's stupendous—it's unique—I don't believe it's ever been thought of before—Oh, boy, it'll be the greatest scoop in the history of movie publicity. . . ."

Which was why, that same evening, Chips gave Miss Lydia Jones the news that Randolph Renny was staying in Brookfield at the Royal Hotel. He decided that if there were to be a scoop at all (whatever a scoop was), Brookfield, as represented by the *Brookfield Gazette* and by its social reporter, should have it. And thus it came about that Miss Jones began her column of gossip ambiguously, ungrammatically, yet in substance correctly with the words: "Coming out of the Royal Hotel the other day, who should I espy but Randolph Renny. . . ."

It only remains to add that the following term Renny's son began his career at Brookfield School, and, during a preliminary interview with Chips, remarked: "Of course you know who my father is, don't you, sir?"

"I do, my boy," Chips answered. "But—umph—you need have no fear—on *that* account. We all know—but at Brookfield—umph—we do not care. . . ."

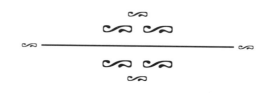

They say that old schoolmasters get into a rut, that it takes a young man to supply new ideas. Perhaps so; and it is true enough that Chips, in his seventieth year, was giving pretty much the same Latin lessons as he had given in his fiftieth or his thirtieth. "The use of—umph—the Supine in 'u,' Richards," said Chips, from his desk in the fourth-form room, "seems to have escaped your notice—umph—and that—umph— can only be ascribed to the Supine in You!" Laughter . . . and if some young man could have done it better, let us give him a cheer, for he is probably doing it better, or trying to—at Brookfield now.

But in 1917, that desperate year darkening toward its close, there were no young men at Brookfield. There was a strange gap between boyhood and age, between the noisy challenge of fourth-formers and the weary glances of elderly overworked men; and only Chips, oldest and most overworked of them all, knew how to bridge that gap with something eternally boyish in himself.

Besides, ideas did come to him—once, for instance, as he was sitting at his desk in the Head's study, that more illustrious desk to which, after his retirement in 1913, he had been summoned as youths were being summoned elsewhere. (But his own service, he often said, was "acting" rather than "active"; and that, with the little "umph—umph" that had become a mannerism with him, was a joke at the expense of his official status of "acting headmaster.")

The idea came because a tall air-browned soldier knocked at the study door during the hour devoted to what Chips called his "acting," strode colossally over the threadbare carpet, and, with a mixture of extreme shyness and bursting cordiality, stood grinning in front of the desk. "Hullo, sir. Thought I'd give you a call while I was hereabouts. And I'll bet you don't know who I am!"

And Chips, adjusting his spectacles in a room already dim with November fog, blinked a little, and—after five seconds—answered: "Oh yes . . . it's—umph—it's Greenaway, isn't it?"

"Well, I guess that's one on me! You've got it right first time, sir! How on earth d'you manage it—Pelmanism or something?"

Chips shook his head with a slow smile. "No . . . no . . . I just—umph—remember. . . . I just remember. . . ." But he was a little saddened, because he had never taken so long to remember before, and he wondered if it were his eyesight or his memory that was beginning to fail; but perhaps, after all, only his eyes, for he added: "You were here in—umph—let me see—in nineteen hundred, eh? Well, how are you, my boy? Umph—you won't mind if— umph—I call you that, will you? . . . Sit down and talk to me. I'm—umph—delighted to see you again. Still— umph—imitating the farmyard?"

"Goodness—you remember *that*, too? You're a

wonder. . . . I've turned Canadian—went out there in nineteen—oh—seven—got my own ranch—found quite a lot of new animals to imitate. . . . Now I'm over with the battalion, and by the freakiest chance we've been sent here to camp. Quite a thriving military centre, Brookfield just now. I met another fellow the other day who used to be in your fourth form—English fellow named Wallingford."

"Wallingford . . . there was only one Wallingford. A quiet boy—umph—with red hair. . . ."

"That's right—it's still red, what's left of it. He asked me to remember him to you. Too shy to come around. I guess there's quite a few Brookfield men stationed here feel the same. School's a strange place when you've left it a dozen years—makes you feel your age when you don't come across a single face you can remember."

"Except mine—umph—eh?"

"Sure . . . and you don't look a day older. But I thought I saw in the papers you'd retired—quite a time ago?"

"So I had, my boy. . . . " And then came the little joke about the "acting service."

The idea came later, when Greenaway, having stayed to lunch in the School Dining Hall, had returned to camp, and when Chips, pleased as he always was by such an encounter, was resting and musing over his afternoon cup of tea. The idea came to him with sudden breathtaking excitement, as a young man may realize that he is in love, or as a poet may think of a lovely line. He would have a party, a Christmas party; there should be no more of that shyness; the men who had once been to Brookfield should meet the boys who were still there; all should meet and mix in the School Hall for an end-of-term party . . . a supper, the best that wartime catering could provide . . . a few songs . . . nonsense for those who liked nonsense, talk and gossip for those who preferred it . . . a few simple toasts, perhaps, and no speeches; nothing formal; everything to make the occasion gay and happy . . . his own party, and his own idea of a party.

It grew bright in his eyes as he thought of it, the details assembled into a rich unity; and by the time he went back to his rooms at Mrs. Wickett's, across the road from the School, it was like good news that he could no longer keep to himself. "Mrs. Wickett," he said, when she came in with his evening meal, "I've had an idea. . . ."

She was rather less enthusiastic than he had hoped. "Mind ye don't tire yeself, that's all," she commented. "There'll be a lot of work arranging a thing of that sort, and if you was to ask me, sir, you're a bit past the age for giving parties!"

"Past it, Mrs. Wickett? Why—umph—I've only just reached it!"

And the smile he gave her faded, as it so often did, into the private smile of reminiscence; he was thinking that he was really the right age because, as a young man, he would have been far too scared and worried to tackle such an enterprise at all. How he had fidgeted, in those days, over whether he ought to put on a white tie or a black tie for some function, whether he ought to shake hands with Mr. So-and-so, whether he would say the right thing in his speech . . . but now, thank heaven, he didn't care, and one of the lovely joys of growing old was to add to this list of trivial things one didn't care about, so that one had more time to care for the things that were not trivial.

"I shall count on you—umph—to help me, Mrs. Wickett. . . . Some of your famous meat-and-potato pies—umph—eh?"

"With wartime flour and strict rations of meat!" answered Mrs. Wickett in pitying scorn. But there were ways and means, and Chips knew that neither wars nor governments would be allowed to frustrate Mrs. Wickett in her search for them. She was *that* sort of an ally.

The next morning the idea was still so strong in him that he dropped a hint to his favorite fourth form and within an hour the rumor was all over the School—"Old Chips is going to give a party!"—"Have you heard the latest—Chips is having a party on the last day of term— a Christmas party"—"Everybody's invited . . . and also some old boys from the camps." This last was added, if at all, as an afterthought; for schoolboys are not really interested in old boys, except on Speech Days or unless they happen to be brothers. Their lack of interest is part of their lack of worry over the future, which is a natural thing—and in 1917 a good thing, too. For then at Brookfield there were boys who were to die within a year; and they were quite happy, playing rugger and conjugating verbs and reading the War news, only half aware that the last concerned them any more than the second, or as much as the first.

So the idea of the party was launched upon a boisterously welcoming world, and in that welcome Chips found more than compensation for extra work; he found a secret sunshine that warmed and comforted him during those sad November days. Indeed, he tremendously enjoyed the planning and discussion and settlement of all the difficult details—the writing of personal invitations, the wheedling of tradesmen into promising precious food, the building up of the whole evening's programme into what, on paper and in anticipation, was already a huge success. And fourth-formers found it enticingly easy, as the term-end drew near, to switch over from conversation about such dull matters as *Cæsar's Gallic War* and the use of the Supine in "u." "*Ut omnes conjurarent.* . . . Oh, I say, sir, that reminds me, do you think we could have any conjuring at the Party? I know a few tricks, sir. . . ."

"Tricks, eh, Wilmer? And evidently—umph—one of those tricks is—umph—not to prepare your work! *Conjuro* doesn't mean 'conjure.' . . ."

"I know, sir, but it reminded me. Do you think I *could* do a few conjuring tricks?"

"Well, well—umph—"

And then of course the lesson was ruined and everyone began to talk about the Party. But no—not ruined. It was the world, the world outside Brookfield, that was nearly in ruins. Beyond the quiet mists of the fen country men in their millions were crouching in frozen mud, starving and thirsting in deserts, drowning in angry seas and swooping to death in midair, fretting in hospitals far from home. So that at Brookfield, even at Brookfield, the Supine in "u" lost ground as a subject of topical discussion; it gave up part of its ancient ghost, and into that place, unbidden but also unforbidden, came Chips's Christmas Party. It was fun to talk about that, to plan more schemes about it, to lure Chips on to chatting, gossiping, telling you things about Brookfield that had happened years before, things you'd never have known about unless Chips had told you them.

"Do you think Jones Tertius could play his mouth organ at the Party, sir? He's awfully good at it."

"I *could* fix the electric lights to make a sort of footlights, sir, in front of the piano—don't you think that would be a good idea?"

"My brother's got a farm, sir, he's promised to send us some real butter. . . ."

And as he sat there at his desk, with suggestions and offers pouring in on him faster than he could deal with them all, he felt that history was not only made by guns and conquests, but by every pleasant thing that stays in memory after it has once happened, and that his Party would so stay, would be remembered at Brookfield as long as—say—the strange revisitation of Mr. Amberley, Mr. Amberley who came back from South America and gave every boy ten shillings to spend at the tuck-shop. "Umph—yes—Mr. Amberley—a good many years ago that was."

"Oh, do tell us about Mr. Amberley, sir."

"Well, you see—umph—Mr. Amberley was once a master here—quite a young man—and not, I fear, very good at dealing with your—umph—ruffianly predecessors. [Laughter] Your father, Marston—umph—will remember Mr. Amberley—umph—because he once—umph—umph—inserted a small snake in the lining of Mr. Amberley's hat. . . . [Laughter] Quite a harmless variety, of course . . . and so—umph—was Mr. Amberley. . . . [Laughter] And then—after his first term—Mr. Amberley very wisely went to South America, where—umph—he was much more successful in forecasting the future price of—umph—nitrates, I think it was. So that when he came back to see us he was—umph—quite a rich man. . . . Bless me, there's the bell—we don't seem to have done very much—umph—this morning. . . ."

"But about the Party, sir—do you think I *could* fix the electric lights, sir?"

"Well, Richards, if you'll undertake not to blow us all up—"

The day came nearer. Three weeks off. A fortnight off. Then "Wednesday week." And on the Thursday the School was to disperse for the Christmas holidays. Brook-field was on rising tiptoe with the pure eagerness of anticipation. When you grow older you miss that eager-ness; life may be happy, you may have health and wealth and love and success, but the odds are that you never look forward as you once did to a single golden day, you never count the hours to it, you never see some moment ahead beckoning like a goddess across a fourth dimen-sion. But Brookfield did, and does still; and so, as that autumn term dragged to an end, the tension rose; the Big Hall took on a faintly roguish air with its unusual em-bellishments of holly and paper festoons; mysterious sounds of practice and rehearsal came from the music rooms; eager discussions were held in the kitchens be-tween staff and housekeeper and Chips.

Because it was so clearly going to be a grand success. Eleven old boys in the neighboring military camps had accepted invitations, and four walking cases from local hospitals; fifteen representatives of the Brookfield that Chips remembered, chance-chosen by the hazards of war. And this timely meeting of boys and men, if Chips allowed himself to dream about it, became something epic in his vision, the closer knitting of a fabric stronger, be-cause more lasting than war. He could not have put much of this into words, and would not even if he could; but the feeling was in him, giving joy to every detail. And the details came crowding in. Richards had contrived an elaborate electrical dodge for lighting up the piano. Greenaway would give his celebrated farmyard imitations. And Chips himself told Mrs. Wickett to look over the dinner suit that he had not worn for years and that smelt of age and camphor.

And then, on a certain Sunday morning in December, an odd thing happened during the School Chapel service— in the middle of a sermon about the disputed authorship of one of the books of the Old Testament. Brookfield, plainly, was not interested in the dispute and definitely declined to take sides in it; you could tell that from the rows of faces in the pews. But all at once, quite astonishingly, something happened that interested Brookfield a great deal; Attwood Primus, commonly called Longlegs, suddenly fainted and, after slipping to the floor with a reverberating crash, had to be dragged out by hastily roused prefects. During the last hymn conversation buzzed excitedly, and (to the tune of "For All the Saints") it was confidently rumored that Attwood was dead.

Attwood, however, was not dead (and is not dead yet); but he was in the sickroom with a temperature of a hundred and two, and before lights-out that same Sunday evening five others had joined him. The next day came seventeen more. Chips, very calm in such an emergency,

Attwood Primus . . . suddenly fainted . . . slipping to
the floor with a reverberating crash.

sat late in consultation with Merivale, the School doctor. With the result that on the following morning Brookfield was alive with the most intoxicating rumor that even a school can ever have.

"I say, heard the latest?—we're breaking up tomorrow instead of Thursday week—someone heard Chips talking to Merivale—"

"It's the 'flu—it's in all the army camps and Longlegs got it from his cousin, who's in one of them—good old Longlegs—"

"Special orders from the War Office—so they say— Nurse told me—"

"Chips has sent down to the bank for journey money—"

"I say—ten days' extra hols—what luck!"

And—in an instant—in less than an instant—the Party was forgotten. Perhaps the conjurer and the mouth-organist gave it a passing thought, perhaps even a thought of wasted planning and unapplauded prowess; but even in them regret was swamped by the overmastering joy of Going Home. Which was only natural. Chips, whose home was Brookfield, knew how natural it was. And so, as he sat at his window in the early morning and watched the taxis curving to and fro through the gateway, he smiled.

He spent Christmas, as he had so often done, in his rooms across the road. There were no visitors, but he was fairly busy. There had been a few details of cancellation to put in order; the promised gifts of food were transferred to hospitals; outside guests were notified that owing to . . . etc., etc., it was much regretted that the Party could not be held. But the decorations remained in the Hall, half finished, and Richards's vaunted footlights, in an embryo stage of dangling flex, impeded the progress of anyone who might seek to mount the platform; but no one did. Then the last of the sickroom unfortunates recovered and went home, shaking hands with Chips as the latter doled out money for the train fare. "Happy Christmas, sir."

"Thank you, Tunstall—umph—and the same to you, my boy."

Christmas Eve brought rain in the late afternoon; it had been a cold day with gray scudding clouds. No school bell sounded across the air, and that to Chips gave a curious impression of timelessness, so that when he sat by the fire and read the paper the moments swam easily toward the dinner hour. "You'll join me, Mrs. Wickett, in—umph—a glass of wine?" he had said, and she had answered, with familiar reluctance: "Oh dear, I dunno as I ought, sir; it does go to me head so."

But she did, of course, and in that little room, with the old-fashioned Victorian furniture and the red-and-blue carpet and the photographs of School groups on the walls, Chips made light of any disappointment that was in him.

"Well, sir, if you was to ask me, I'd say it was proper

"You'll join me, Mrs. Wickett, in—umph—a glass of wine?"

Providence, it was, for it's my belief the fuss of it all would have knocked you up—that it would, and Doctor Merivale said the same, knowin' what a lively set-to them boys was going to make of it."

"*Were* they, Mrs. Wickett? Umph—umph—well, they're all enjoying their own parties—now—more than—umph—they'd have enjoyed anything here—umph—that's very certain!"

"Oh no, sir, I don't think that, sir."

"Mrs. Wickett—umph—no normal healthy-minded boy—umph—ever wants to stay at school a moment longer than he needs—umph—and I'm glad to say that my boys are—umph—almost *excessively* normal! When is it that they're due back—January 15—umph—eh?"

"That's right, sir. Term begins on the fifteenth."

"Umph—three weeks more."

After dinner he decided to write some letters, and as he had left an address book in his school desk he walked across the road through the gusty rain and unlocked his way into the chilly rooms and corridors where his feet guided him unerringly. A strange place, an empty school. Full of ghosts, full of echoes of voices, full of that sad smell of stale ink, varnish, and the carbolic soap that the charwomen used. In every classroom a scrap of writing on the blackboard, words or figures, some last thing done before the world lost its inhabitants. And on a whitewashed wall in a deserted corridor Chips saw, roughly scrawled in pencil, what looked at first to be some odd mathematical calculation:

17
16
15
14
13
12
11
10
9

Which, of course, at second glance he perfectly understood; nay more, he could imagine the joy of the eager calculator when, after that memorable Sunday, the last eight digits of the progression had been spared him! And possibly that same calculator, at this very moment on Christmas Eve, was giving a rueful thought to the date that lay ahead—January 15—"only three more weeks!" Boys were like that.

He found his book and relocked the doors; then, back in Mrs. Wickett's house again, he wrote his letters. Like most of his, they were written to old boys of the School, and like most letters to old boys they were now addressed to camps and armies throughout the world. Chips was not a particularly good letter writer. His jokes came to him only in speech; in letters he was always very simple and direct and (if you thought so) rather dull. Indeed, one of their recipients (a much cleverer man than Chips) had once called them affectionately "the letters of a schoolmaster by a schoolboy." Just this sort of thing:

"DEAR BRADLEY—I am very glad to hear you are getting on well after your bad smash. We have had a pretty fair term, on the whole (beat Barnhurst twice at rugger), but an epidemic of 'flu attacked us near the end, interfering with the House matches and one or two other affairs. We broke up ten days early on account of this. Mr. Godley has been called up, despite his age and health, so we are understaffed again. We had an air raid in October, but no one at the School was hurt. If you get leave and can spare the time, do come and see me here. We begin term on January 15. . . ."

Chips wrote several of these letters; then he sat by the fire over his evening cup of tea. All that he had not said, and could never say or write, flooded his mind at the thought of a world so full of bloodshed and peril; and then, in answer, came the thought of those boys who might, by happier chance, miss such peril as carelessly and as cheerfully as they had missed his Party. And he prayed, seated and silent: God, bring peace on earth . . . goodwill to men and boys. . . .

"Will ye be wantin' anything more, sir?"

"No thank you, Mrs. Wickett."

"Happy Christmas to you, sir."

"And the same—umph—to you, Mrs. Wickett."

"Thank you, sir. It don't seem long, sir, since—"

Mrs. Wickett always had to say that it didn't seem long since last Christmas, or last Good Friday, or last Sports Day, or some other annual occasion. Chips smiled as she did so—a gentle smile, for there was something in his mind that was always tolerant of tradition. We have our ways, and if we are good folk our ways are fondly endured. "Time goes so quickly, sir, you 'ardly know where you are. Only another three weeks and we'll 'ave the beginning of term again. . . ."

"Yes—umph—only another three weeks," answered Chips. And that, of course, was probably what the boys were saying. But Chips, thinking of those lonely classrooms, meant it differently.

Afterword

When Good-bye, Mr. Chips *first appeared in America, it was published to great acclaim in* The Atlantic Monthly *magazine. Four years later James Hilton's byline could again be found on the* Atlantic's *pages. In an essay in the July 1938 issue, the author described the inspiration for his most memorable character and reflected on his own public schooling. But underlying the warm remembrances was another far less genial subject. For in 1938 England was on the brink of World War II. And James Hilton, whose boyhood had been shadowed by World War I, saw only too clearly the dark days that lay ahead. Here is an excerpt from that article.*

What Mr. Chips Taught Me

If I use the word "I" a good deal in these pages, it is not from self-importance, but because I would rather talk about my own school days than generalize about schools. Schooling is perhaps the most universal of all experiences, but it is also one of the most individual. (Here

I am, generalizing already!) No two schools are alike, but more than that—a school with two hundred pupils is really two hundred schools, and among them, almost certainly, are somebody's long-remembered heaven and somebody else's hell. The schools I write of were *my* schools; to others at the same schools at the same time, everything may have been different.

I went to three schools altogether—an elementary school, a grammar school, and a public school. After that, I matriculated at London University and spent four years at Christ's College, Cambridge. Thus, from age six, when my mother led me through suburban streets for presentation to the headmistress of the nearest Infants' Department, up to age twenty-three, when I left Cambridge, the process called my education was going on. Seventeen years—quite a large slice out of a life, when you come to think about it. And yet the ways I have earned my living since—by writing newspaper articles, novels, and film scenarios—were not taught me at any of these schools. Furthermore, though I won scholarships and passed examinations, I do not think I remember more than twenty percent of all I learned during those years, and I do not think I could now scrape through any of the examinations I passed after the age of twelve.

There was no coordination between my three schools and the university. To some extent, I learned what I liked; to a greater extent, my teachers taught me what they liked. At the elementary school, for instance, I spent an hour a week on Botany, which was an excuse for wandering through Epping Forest in charge of a master who regarded the hour as an excuse for a pleasant smoke in the open air. The result is that Botany to me today stands for just a few words like calyx, stamen, and capillary attraction, plus the memory of lovely hours amidst trees and bracken. I do not complain.

The only school learning of which I remember a good deal belongs to English Literature, History, and Music; but even in these fields my knowledge is roving rather than academic, and I could no longer discuss with any degree of accuracy the debt of Shakespeare to Saxo Grammaticus. To make up for all I have forgotten, there is this that I have acquired, and I call it sophistication, since it is not quite the same thing as learning. It is the armor of doubt in an age when too many people are certain.

The elementary school was in one of the huge suburbs of northeast London. Whenever nowadays I pass by that school, I realize what an age it is since I breathed its prevalent smell of ink, strong soap, and wet clothes. Just over a quarter of a century, to be precise, but it cannot be measured by that reckoning. The world today looks back on the pre-War world as a traveler may look back through a railway tunnel to the receding pinpoint of light in the distance. It is more than the past; it is already a legend.

To this legend my earliest recollections of school life

belong. My father was the headmaster of another school in the same town, and I was a good deal petted and favored by his colleagues. There were quite a few dirty and ragged boys in the class of seventy or so; the school itself was badly heated and badly lit; schoolbooks were worn and smeary because every boy had to follow the words with his finger as he read—an excusable rule, for it was the only way the teacher could see at a glance if his multitude were all paying attention. He was certainly not to blame because I found his reading lessons a bore. At the time that I was spelling out "cat-sat-on-the-mat" stuff at school, I was racing through Dickens, Thackeray, and Jules Verne at home.

From the elementary school I went to a grammar school in the same suburb. I had the luck to have for a form master a man who was very deaf. I call it luck because he was an excellent teacher and would probably have attached himself to a much better school but for his affliction. As it was, his discipline was the best in the school.

I was devoted to that man. His frown could spoil my day; his rare slanting smile could light it up. I was conceited enough to think that he took some special interest in me, just because he read out my essays publicly to the class; and after I sent him in an essay, I used to picture the excitement he must feel on reading it. It did not occur to me that, like most good professionals, he did his job conscientiously but without hysterical enthusiasm, and that during out-of-school hours he would rather have a drink and a chat with a friend than read the best school-boy's essay ever written.

I cannot imagine any more desperate situation for a school than the one in which this grammar school found itself. Flanked on one side by a pickle factory, it shared its other aspects between the laundry of the municipal baths and a busy thoroughfare lined by market stalls. I grew used to the smell of chutney and steaming bath towels, to the cries of costers selling oranges and cough drops, and it was fun to step out of the classroom on winter evenings and search a book barrow lit by naphtha flares or listen to a Hindu peddling a corn cure.

I probably learned more in the street than I did in the school, but I worked hard there, chiefly because home-work was piled on by various masters acting independently of each other. I was a quick worker, but often I did not finish till nearly midnight, and how the slower workers managed I can only imagine.

It is perhaps a pity that the average school curriculum fits a pupil for one profession better than any other—that of schoolmastering. It is a pity because the clever school-boy is tempted into the only profession in which his store of knowledge is of immediate practical value in getting him a job, and is then tempted to emphasize the value of passing on precisely that same knowledge to others. The circle is vexatious, but I would not call it vicious, because I do not think that the whole or even the chief value of a schoolmaster can be measured by the knowledge he imparts. Much of that knowledge will be forgotten anyway, and far more easily than the influence of a cultured and liberal-minded personality. Indeed, in a world in which practical people are so busy doing things that had better not be done at all, there may even be some advantage in the sheer mundane uselessness of a classical education. Better the vagaries of *tollo* than those of a new poison gas; better to learn and forget our Latin verbs than to learn and remember our experimental chemistry; better by far we should forget and smile than that we should remember and be sad.

So I defend (somewhat tepidly) a classical education. It is of small practical value in a world whose practical values are mostly wrong; it is "waste time" in a world whose time had better be wasted than spent in most of its present activities. My Mr. Chips, who went on with his Latin lesson while the Zeppelins were dropping bombs, was aware that he was "wasting" the possibly last moments of himself and his pupils, but he believed that he was wasting them with dignity and without malice.

The War broke out while I was still at the suburban grammar school; during that last lovely June of the pre-War era, I had won a scholarship to a public school in Hertfordshire. I remember visiting a charming little country town and being quartered there at a temperance hotel in company with other entrants.

But I never saw the place again, because my father,

poring over the prospectus, discovered that the school possessed a rifle range and an Officers' Training Corps— symbols of the War that, above all things, he hated. He had been a pacifist long before he ever called himself one (indeed, he never liked the term), and it is literally true to say that he would not hurt a fly—for my mother could never use a fly swatter if he was in the same room. Yet I know that if anyone had broken into our house and attacked my mother or me, it would have been no problem at all to my father; he would have died in battle.

I was just fourteen then—the age at which most boys in England leave school and go to work. But my father was still dallying with the notion of a public school for me, and soon conceived that, since he could not make up his mind, I should choose a school for myself. So I toured England on this eccentric but interesting quest and learned how to work out train journeys from York to Cheltenham and from Brighton to Sherborne, how to pick good but cheap hotels in small towns, and how to convince a headmaster that if I didn't get a good impression of his school, I should unhesitatingly cross it off my list.

Eventually I spent a weekend at Cambridge and liked the town and university atmosphere so much that I finally chose a school there, despite the fact that the school possessed both the rifle range and the cadet corps. Relying on the fact that my father was both forgetful and unobservant, I said nothing about this at home, got myself entered for the school, and joined it halfway through the summer term of 1915.

I was not a typical schoolboy, and the fact that I was happy at (shall we say?) Brookfield argues that the school tolerated me even more generously than I tolerated it. I did not join the almost compulsory Officers' Training Corps, despite the fact that the years were 1914–1918. My reasons for keeping out were simply that I disliked military training and had no aptitude for it. Lest readers should picture my stand as a heroic one, I should add that it was really no stand at all: nobody persecuted me; if anyone had, no doubt I should have joined.

I had many acquaintances at Brookfield, and a few close friends with whom my relationship was as unselfish as any I have experienced since in my life. I do not think I had any particular enemies, and I got on well enough with authority. I played the piano dashingly rather than accurately at speech-day concerts, breakfasted with the Head once a term, argued for or against capital punishment (I forget which) in the school debating society, and cycled many windy miles along the fenland lanes.

Looking back on those days, I see that they had an epic quality. Behind the murmur of genitive plurals in dusty classrooms and the plick-plock of cricket balls in the summer sunshine, there was always the rumble of guns, the guns that were destroying the world that Brookfield had made and that had made Brookfield. Sometimes these guns were actually audible, or we fancied they were; every weekday there was a rush to the news-papers, every Sunday a batch of names read out to stilled listeners. The careful assessments of schoolmasters were blotted out by larger and wilder markings; a boy who had been expelled returned as a hero with medals; offenders gated for cigarette smoking in January were dropping bombs from the sky in December. Slowly, inch by inch, the tide of War lapped to the gates of our seclusion; play-ing fields were ploughed up for drill grounds; cadet corps duties took precedence over classroom studies; the school that had prepared so many beloved generations for life was preparing this one, equally beloved, for death.

On Sundays we attended Chapel and heard sermons that preached brotherly love and forgiveness of our en-emies. On Mondays we watched cadets on the football field bayoneting sacks with special aim for vital parts of the human body. I wondered endlessly whether Sunday's or Monday's behaviour were the more hypocritical. I have changed my attitude since. That Brookfield declined to rationalize warfare into its code of ethics while at the same time sending its sons to fight and die seems to me now to have been pardonably illogical and creditably inconsis-tent. I can see that countries where high ideals are preached but not practised are at least better off than countries in which low ideals are both preached *and* practised.

Many of us at Brookfield, like myself, were young—*just* too young—to see actual service in the War; yet dur-ing our last school years we lived under its shadow. There is hardly a big event of those years that I do not associate with a Brookfield scene: Kitchener's death reminds me of cricketers hearing the news as they fastened pads in the pavilion; the Russian Revolution gives me the voice of a man, now dead, who talked about it instead of giving his usual geography lesson; the *Lusitania* sinking reminds me of the first headlines read hastily over a master's shoulder at breakfast. I composed a sonnet on the Russian Revolution, which my father sent to the editor of the London *Daily News,* eliciting from him the comment that it "showed merit." I also wrote a poem on the *Lusitania,* which appeared in the *Cambridge Magazine,* a pacifist weekly.

These things I recount not for vainglory (for they were not particularly good poems), but to reveal something of the mood of Brookfield, in which a boy could be eccentric enough to write poetry and subversive enough to write pacifist and revolutionary poetry without being either persecuted or ostracized. As a matter of fact, I was editor of the school magazine, and wrote for it articles, stories, and poems of all kinds. Nobody tried to censor them; nobody tried to depose or harass me. Looking back on this genial indifference, it seems to me that Brookfield in wartime was not only less barbarian than the world outside it, but also less barbarian than many institutions in what we have since chosen to call peacetime.

I do not know whether this spirit obtained at other schools besides Brookfield. Probably at some it did and at others it didn't. But I stress it because the quality of an institution can be tested by the extent to which it withstands attack. Granted that during the War all civilized institutions were subtly contaminated, which of them passed such a test most creditably?

Mr. Chips, if he were alive (and I have reason to believe he is, in a few schools), could still give the same lessons as in 1908 (not an ideal educational programme, but one that at least attests the durability of a tradition). No upstart authority has yet compelled him to click his heels and begin the day with juju incantations of *Heils* and *Vivas*. He can still say, without fear of rubber truncheons: "Umph—Mr. Neville Chamberlain—umph—I used to know his father when he was the wild man of Born—I mean Birmingham . . . but his sons have turned—umph—respectable. . . ."

This spirit of free criticism, even if it expresses itself no more momentously than as a classroom squib, is the sort of thing that makes English conservatives liberal and keeps English socialists conservative. It is the spirit that made Mr. Chips protest amidst the bomb explosions: "These things that have mattered for a thousand years are not going to be snuffed out because some stink-merchant invents a new kind of mischief."

Do not think I am blind to the faults of the age of which Mr. Chips and his type were the product as well as the makers. Its imperialism was smug, hypocritical, and predatory. Its laissez-faire capitalism resulted in such horrors as child slavery in factories. But one fact does emerge from the period beginning with the Queen's accession and ending with her death—that it was possible for a man in Western Europe to look around his world and believe that it was getting better. He could see the spread of freedom in thought and speech. He could watch the transplantation of parliamentary government into lands where, though it might not wholly suit the soil, few doubted it would eventually flourish. A man and his son and his son's son might live and die in the belief that the world would not witness certain things again.

All of which may sound a huge digression. But for me it is not so. I cannot think of my school days without the image of that incredible background—Zeppelins droning over sleeping villages, Latin lessons from which boys stepped into the brief lordliness of a second-lieutenancy on the Somme. I cannot forget the soft fenland rain beginning to fall on Cambridge streets at dusk, with old men fumbling in and out of bookshops, and young men, spent after route marches, scampering over ancient quadrangles.

Those days were history, but most of us were too young to be historians, too young to disassociate the trivial from the momentous—gnarled desks and War headlines, photogravure generals and the school butler who stood at the foot of the dormitory staircase and at lights-out warned sepulchrally, "Time, gentlemen, Time." It was Time in a way that so many of us could not realize. That warning marked the days during which, on an average, ten thousand men were killed

Mr. Chips would walk between the lines of beds in the dormitory and turn out the lights. He was an old man then. School days are a microcosm of life—the boy is born the day he enters the school and dies the day he leaves it: in between are youth, middle age, and the elderly respectability of the sixth form. But outside this cycle stands the schoolmaster, remembering faces and incidents as a god might remember history. An old schoolmaster, if he is well liked and has dignity, is like a god. You can joke about him behind his back, but you must acknowledge him to his face while you love him a little carelessly in your hearts.

There was no single schoolmaster I ever knew who was entirely Mr. Chips, but there were several who had certain of his attributes and achieved that best reward of a well-spent life—to grow old beloved. One of them was my father. He did not train aristocrats to govern the Empire or plutocrats to run their fathers' businesses, but he employed his wise and sweetening influence just as valuably among the thousands of elementary schoolboys who knew and know him still in a London suburb.

James Hilton
1938